The Comeback

CAMPUS CONFESSIONS
BOOK THREE

CYNTHIA GUNDERSON

With Gratitude

Editing and Critique
Scott Gunderson, Sue Prince

Cover Design
Ink and Veil

I can't believe we're at the last book in the Campus Confessions series! After Logan's fall from grace in The Breakaway, I knew I had to bring him back. I just wasn't sure how. He was fairly hateable in book 1, but I've always had a soft spot for him.

When we're young, we really only know what's been modeled for us, and when Logan showed up and apologized to Shar, I saw that as his origin story, not his endpoint. Add in that as a mother of three boys, I've been on a personal war path to change the perceptions we have culturally about men and intimacy, especially where sex is concerned.

I bring that up because there is a scene in this book that goes a little beyond my typical closed door. Nothing explicit as usual, but I couldn't stop before a particular conversation took place. Just like women can't always predict how their bodies will respond in intimate situations, men don't always have control either. The idea that sex is easy for men, that they get whatever they want (that's stated multiple times about Logan in prior books) is perpetuated constantly, but maybe we need to step back and realize that we both want the same thing. And we only find it together.

That's what I wanted Logan and Crystal to figure out. That

true love and intimacy require risk. You can't have one without the other.

Here's to the hard conversations. The admissions. The vulnerability.

Here's to what it takes to love.

xo Cindy

P.S. Remember that when you get to the end of this book and you want more…Canadian Played is an eight book epilogue. Just saying.

Prologue

VOICEMAIL LEFT FOR LOGAN KEMP BY CRYSTAL MACMILLAN
NOVEMBER 1ST, 1995

"Hey, Logan. Sorry I haven't called before now, but you asked me to let you know when Rob and Shar's baby was here, and he's not here yet, I'll say that first. But we think he'll be arriving in the next week or so. Not totally sure, but Shar's been having contractions. Sorry, probably more than you want to know. Uh . . . yeah. Just wanted to keep you in the loop. Hope you're doing well, and all the stuff with the Blizzard is good. I don't know, this is weird right? We're old enough to have friends having babies. Well, probably weirder for you. Sorry, I shouldn't have said that, I . . . well. You know what I mean. Kay, bye Logan."

VOICEMAIL LEFT FOR CRYSTAL MACMILLAN BY LOGAN KEMP
NOVEMBER 2ND, 1995

"Hey. Thanks for the message, and sorry I missed you. Had a pre-season game. You probably know that, er, maybe not? Not sure if you

follow the Blizzard. I wouldn't expect you to, not because I'm playing there or anything. But really good to hear from you. It's crazy being back in Calgary but not really being back. If that makes sense? I see my family and everything, but all my friends are there at Douglas. Yeah. All of that is pretty weird, but it's my fault it's weirder for me, so you don't need to apologize. Just saying it how it is, I guess. Uh . . . I don't know what Shar and Rob need, so if you have any ideas. I searched on the web and saw maybe diapers would be a good idea. Not sure if they have a brand they like or something—no, they haven't even tried them yet, right? How could they? Shar's not picky anyway, but . . . I don't know, maybe she is. So, yeah. Let me know if you have any ideas. You can email me if that's easier? LKeatsice@hotmail.com. My old one, not my school email. I don't know why I said that, you probably didn't ever have my email anyway. Okay. See ya later. And thanks again. Bye."

From: Crystal MacMillan cmacmillan@douglasu.org
To: Logan Kemp LKeatsice@hotmail.com
Date: November 7, 1995, 10:42 AM
Subject: Gift for Rob and Shar

Hey, I asked Shar whether they needed anything specific. And she told me about this pillow that was supposed to be really great. But I called around to a couple of stores, and I think they might only sell them in the States. My parents wanted to do something for her, and my mom is driving down to Kalispell for my brother's hockey tournament this weekend, so I'm going to have her grab it.

Shar told me her parents got them a small freezer, so Maddie and I were thinking about getting some meals together for them for after the baby comes. I'm a terrible cook, so probably store-bought. But that's something you could help with, too, if you want.

Or, yeah, diapers and wipes. Sorry. That's probably not very exciting. I didn't mention you specifically because there were a couple of people asking, but I realized I didn't know if you wanted them to know you were getting them something. I meant to tell Shar I talked to you after the baby shower, but didn't want to make things more awkward. You tell me. I don't have to say anything if you don't want me to.

This might be prying . . . but have you talked to Rob at all since you came back? Have you talked to any of the guys? You don't have to answer if you don't want to. Let me know if you want to contribute to the meals or something.

Crystal

From: Logan Kemp LKeatsice@hotmail.com
To: Crystal MacMillan cmacmillan@douglasu.org
Date: November 13, 1995, 9:16 PM
Subject: Re: Gift for Rob and Shar

Hey. Thanks for that. I'd love to give some money for meals, and I'll also buy some diapers. I'm cool if they know it's from me. I'll give a card or something with the diapers. I'm not trying to be anonymous. My ego's too big for that, but I'm sure you already know that. Just kidding (kind of).

Are you guys going shopping at some point? Maybe I could meet you there and pay? Is that weird? Sorry. I don't want to put you in an awkward situation, but it would be great to see people from Douglas. I miss everyone. I'm super busy and playing hockey, so life is good. But, you know, like you said, everybody's going to be moving in different directions soon. Wild.

Logan

P.S. Talked to Rob once. Haven't caught up with the rest of the team yet.

CHAPTER
One

GROCERY SHOPPING with hockey players was a bad idea under the best of circumstances. Spending time with a one-time faculty member and Sharla's ex immediately disqualified this evening as a good time, and yet here I was pushing a squeaky cart into Co-op. At least Maddie was there. My one saving grace.

The automatic doors sighed open for Chase and Logan, burping out warm bakery air over the four of us. Fluorescent lights hummed. A little kid in a puffy parka zoomed past in boots, nearly clipping my ankle. Calgary in November turned the entrance to any building into a minefield with people trying to avoid the frigid temps or peanut butter snow slush (if we were lucky).

"Crystal!" Maddie waved me away from the produce section.

"Freezer aisle?" Chase, the one-time assistant coach for the Douglas University Outlaws and Maddie's forever person, pulled the cart from my hands.

"Nice of you to wait until we were inside," I teased, letting him push.

"The metal's still threatening to fuse to my skin. It counts."

Maddie huffed a laugh, giving Logan Kemp the side eye as he stopped beside us. That was deserved. Honestly, I probably deserved a look for saying yes to him participating in this little venture.

Logan cheated on Sharla while he was at World Juniors. There. I said it. It was nice of him to want to make amends and support Sharla and Rob, but it was going to take more than diapers and freezer meals to scrub "asshole" from his permanent record.

I started toward the cold section. "Should we shoot for quick food that's edible, preferably not shaped like dinosaurs?"

Maddie fell into step beside me, shimmying out of her peacoat sleeves. "Dinosaur shapes increase compliance in controlled trials," she deadpanned.

Chase's mouth tugged. He reached out and slid his hand under her spiral curls, squeezing the back of her neck.

Ugh. He was obsessed with her. Not that I was mad about it, but watching Chase and Rob fawn over Maddie and Shar was getting to be a little much since I was the permanent fifth wheel in our group at this point.

"We could do lasagna or shepherd's pie. Shar'll actually eat those." Logan pulled his ball cap lower over his face. Baby-blond hair stuck out the back, curling around his ears.

I gave him a look. "I don't think you get to say what Shar will eat or not."

Maddie's eyes widened, but I walked ahead before either of them could say anything. I was as surprised as anyone that I snapped. I'd communicated with Logan a few times over the past few weeks and had been more than cordial. But something about seeing him in person again made Sharla's teary face, her body curled on her bed, pop back up in my mind. Or maybe I was just trying to make it clear to Maddie and Chase that allowing him to come wasn't the same as an invitation to make friendship bracelets.

I wasn't going to treat him like a pariah, especially since Sharla was meant to be with Rob and Logan's poor behaviour may have helped that happen. But had I been a little too nice?

"I deserved that." Logan sped up to walk next to me.

"Yeah. You did." I turned down the aisle for frozen meat. Chase and Maddie trailed behind us with the cart.

The freezer hummed with that constant low drone that made your teeth buzz, and behind the foggy panes, the world of prepared food awaited. Hungry-Man dinners, Salisbury steak, Stouffer's lasagna, and something called a "complete chicken feast," which sounded more like a dare than a meal.

I pulled open one of the doors, the cold air spilling out in a rush that made my fingers ache. They still weren't fully warmed from the parking lot. I snatched two boxes of shepherd's pie and handed them to Maddie to put in the cart. I wasn't going to admit Logan was right about that one, but I also wouldn't withhold one of Shar's favourites.

"And she likes those Michelina's pasta bowls," Maddie said. "Alfredo, not marinara."

Logan wandered to the end of the aisle. While I loaded pasta bowls, he returned with an armful of juice concentrates. "For Rob. He eats these with a spoon."

I grimaced.

"Wait, am I allowed to say what he likes?" Logan asked, his eyebrow raised, and I couldn't tell if he was being serious or not. Logan at Douglas was never serious, and something in my stomach twisted when I realized I hadn't seen him smile once since he got out of his truck tonight.

"That's disgusting." Maddie motioned for him to drop the juices in the cart.

"Shar also used to inhale those frozen spring rolls," he said, squinting at the next section. "The ones in the yellow box."

I shook my head. "She switched to red. The sauce packets are better."

Logan's mouth twitched. "Okay, then."

"What? I'm not—I'm just stating a fact." I marched toward the next door.

"Didn't realize you were so pissed at me. That's all."

"I'm not pissed." I yanked the door open.

"Feels like you're pissed."

I grabbed three red boxes. "Well, I don't know. Seeing you all . . . like this—" I motioned at his waffle-knit, long-sleeved Henley that made it obvious he'd put on at least ten pounds of muscle since we'd last seen each other.

"Like what?" He threw out his arms.

"All successful and shit." I dropped the boxes in the cart.

Logan huffed a laugh. "Ah. I'm a bad person, so the universe should be punishing me?"

Maddie and Chase pushed to the end of the aisle, pretending they didn't hear any of this.

I planted my hands on my hips. "Yeah. Or at least not giving you million-dollar NHL contracts."

"You're right. All professional athletes are standouts in moral and ethical behaviour. I'm the anomaly." Logan took a step closer. "Also, I'm pretty sure Shar won this round." He spun and stalked off after the cart.

Won this round? I practically spluttered as I jogged after him. "What does that mean?"

"Nothing."

"You were the only one competing for—"

"For what?" He turned, glowering at me from under the brim of his hat.

"For . . . *prom king.* Or whatever they called it on that Buffy episode. A popularity contest."

"I know what prom king is."

"Well, I was making sure." I swallowed hard. Logan stood at least a foot taller than me, and I'd never seen him like this. Like something inside him was about to snap. Maybe I shouldn't have kept poking him with a stick. Repeatedly, like a dead squirrel.

He drew a deep breath and exhaled slowly. "I had a lot of issues."

"Had?"

He wet his lips. "Yeah. They're all gone now. I'm perfect."

I scoffed.

Logan opened the freezer door and grabbed a bag of pierogi. "Sharla and Rob were meant for each other from the beginning. I'm not saying that to absolve myself. I know I acted like a dick. But . . . I don't know. Maybe I always knew I wasn't good enough."

I blinked.

He paused and then finished, "Seems like we both got what we wanted."

That comment made me work to pull my heart out of my throat. Sharla wanted Rob, but Logan—

"I got hockey." He hissed, shoving his free hand in his pocket before stepping back, then turned and rounded the end of the aisle. Before he disappeared, he paused and said, "I'm going to get ice cream. Shar likes cookie dough. Unless that's changed, too?"

My jaw dropped at his tone. *Asshole.*

I caught up to him at the whipped toppings. "So, what, this is your way of making things right?" That wasn't going to happen. One couldn't just buy a pint of ice cream to atone for all the crap he'd pulled.

Logan stopped at the next freezer and peered through the glass. "No."

"What is it, then?"

"Like you said. Rob was my best friend." He reached in and pulled out a container of Tillamook. "Despite my cold, dead heart when it comes to relationships, I actually do care about people."

The door fell closed with a thunk. Maddie and Chase appeared at the end of the aisle, and Logan strode toward them, but didn't quite make it.

A guy in a puffer vest let go of his cart and stepped into his path with a starstruck grin. "Hey. You're Logan Kemp, right? From the Blizzard?"

Logan's shoulders tightened an inch. "Yeah." That old smile from Ranchman's came out full force as he extended his hand, but then he thought better of it. Logan wiped his palm on his jeans before shaking. "Nice to meet you. What's your name?"

"Casey." The man held out a Co-op receipt and a pen without a cap, asked for an autograph, and then his wife popped around the corner with a bag of frozen peas and pretended she didn't see what was happening. The blush on her cheeks gave her away.

She performed the whole "Oh, who?" farce fairly well, to her credit.

"Good luck this weekend," Casey said. "We're pullin' for you, bud."

"Thanks." Logan nodded and continued on his way, setting the ice cream in the cart.

"You get that a lot?" I asked once we'd turned into the snack aisle.

"Some. It's Calgary. People are nice about it."

"Still weird, though, right?" Maddie pulled a bag of Doritos from the shelf.

Logan shrugged. "Not that different from Douglas."

Chase laughed and nodded. "Campus celebrities."

That was true. The guys on the Outlaws team couldn't go anywhere after a big win without people trying to be buddy-buddy with them, dig up insider info, or get in their pants.

"It's kind of different." I grabbed a box of chocolate Teddy Grahams and added it to the cart. "But I'm sure there are benefits, right?"

Maddie gave me a look. I was being a brat, but couldn't quite stop it. She read the signs and looped her arm in mine, then strode up the aisle. "Hey, friend. How are you?"

"So good."

She stopped, staring up at the cookies. "You invited him, remember?"

"I was trying to be nice."

"And now you decided to . . . not?"

I blew out a breath, checking to make sure he and Chase weren't listening. They were chatting across the cart. "It's just weird. He's barely talked with Rob. Hasn't reached out to the team. Like, why do all this when you're not even willing to put forth effort with those guys?"

"Uh, it makes perfect sense. The team was pissed about everything. He's probably nervous to talk to them again, and this is something he can do without seeing them face to face."

Oh. Yeah. There was that.

"It's a nice gesture. Even if he's trying to buy his way back into their good graces, at least he's trying," she finished.

"Should've *tried* not to snog other girls at Juniors."

Maddie leaned closer. "How guilty do you think he feels? Do you think we can get him to pay half?"

I snorted. "Whatever, your boyfriend has an actual job. You don't even have to pay for gas anymore."

She pulled her arm free with a scoff. "Uh, I filled up *his* truck today."

"Because you drive it more than he does! Don't you have a car?"

"It's going to snow soon." Maddie grinned and pulled me back to the cart where we caught Logan saying, "Your winger, McTavish—kid's got wheels."

Chase chuckled. "Yeah, he and Leduc are dynamite until they forget they're not shooting for solo careers. Every line change is a soap opera." He turned to Maddie, his face lighting up at the mere sight of her.

Maddie grinned. "Crystal, how about you go and help Logan with the diapers? We'll grab the rest of the snacks and meet you at the front?"

If I thought "grab the rest of the snacks" was a euphemism for "Make out behind the water jugs on the next aisle down," I might not have argued.

I started, "How about—"

"Hey, don't talk back to your mom." Logan smirked and put out an arm like he expected me to take it. As if.

I looked between the two of them. Maddie sidled closer to Chase, and Logan still looked like a butler. He had the cheesy grin and everything.

"Oh my gosh, fine." I didn't take his arm, but I did find it in me to apologize before Maddie had to chastise me again. "Sorry I was rude. It's been a long week."

"Hey, I get it," Logan said as we turned down the baby aisle. "You're losing both your friends."

My breathing hitched, but I quickly recovered. "No, that's—it has nothing to do with that. And I'm not *losing* them."

Logan slowed, his eyes glazing over at the wall of colourful plastic. "Hm. Maybe not."

That concession was worse than an argument. I chewed my lower lip, blinking against the pressure behind my eyes. *Maybe not.* This baby was going to come, then the three of us would be with our respective families for Christmas, and then . . . it would be May before we knew it.

Maddie was pushing full steam ahead with her new Elite League and already had offers for analytics positions from companies scattered throughout Alberta. Chase had his coaching job with the Hitmen, so hopefully that would at least motivate them to stay local.

But was I really going to go over and hang out with them as is? Single? Would we go out to dinner just the three of us? Having Shar and Rob around was better, but it was always painfully obvious that I was the fifth wheel. The loser single friend.

"What are you working on right now?" Logan pulled a pack of size Newborn diapers from the shelf and inspected it.

"What do you mean?"

"Your art. You still do that, right?"

Nothing could have surprised me more than that sentence. "You know I do art?"

Logan nodded. "Wow. So I was that big of a dick." He handed me a pack of diapers, then pulled two more off the shelves. "Do you think two newborns and one in a bigger size?"

"It seems like a lot of diapers."

He handed me another pack. "Don't babies poop like ten times a day or something?"

"That can't be true." That weight on my chest pressed deeper. *What were we even doing?* We were too young for this. For any of it. My fear for Sharla ramped up another ten degrees.

He shoved two more packs under his arm and called it good, motioning toward the front.

I adjusted the packs in my arms and blew out a breath. "You weren't mean or anything. I just didn't think you knew or cared what I was up to."

Logan lowered his head, blocking his face with the brim of his hat, as we passed another couple in the aisle. As much as he said it wasn't different to play for the Blizzard, I never saw him do that on campus.

"I was a little self-centred," he said.

"Again with the past tense."

Logan chuckled, and a smile slipped past my ice queen defences.

"I've been sculpting lately," I answered his earlier question. "Right now I'm working on a series that explores structure and collapse."

"Ah. Obviously. The . . . stuff that holds and then . . . doesn't."

I snorted. "I'll submit that as my thesis."

"What do you want to do with it?" he asked.

"My art?" I shrugged. "Creating's mostly for fun. I want to land a curator or gallery assistant job after graduation."

"Does that pay well?"

I shot him a look. "Nothing pays well compared to your job."

Logan laughed. "How much do you think I make?"

"I saw the press release." It was all over the Calgary papers. $200k annually.

"Did the article mention agent fees? Taxes?"

We rejoined Maddie and Chase in line, their cart loaded like a small nation's supply convoy.

"Wow, look at you using real adult words." Maddie gave Logan a satisfied smirk.

Logan shook his head. "Man. Didn't realize how cush it was hanging with people who think I'm cool. At least Chase gets me."

Chase gave him a fist bump and started unloading the freezer food.

Logan sighed and dropped the diapers on the conveyor belt. "You girls will understand all that finance talk someday."

I slugged him in the shoulder. "I'm older than you."

He winced. "By a month."

"And more educated," Maddie added.

"By a *month*," Logan grumbled. "Or ten."

I wondered whether he was going to finish his degree, but didn't ask. He hadn't seemed all that serious about his classes at Douglas before his big break. Probably hadn't thought twice about it.

The conveyor belt hummed, and Logan shifted the juice tubes forward with the rest of the cold items. He turned to me. "My mom's friend is opening some kind of gallery downtown. Or maybe a museum? I can't remember."

My pulse ticked up. "Really?" Logan's parents were loaded. I wasn't sure what his dad did, but he owned a few places in Calgary, including the townhouse Logan, Shar, and Rob used to live in.

"Yeah. I'll find out the details," he said, pulling out his wallet. "I think his name is Marcus . . . Nieman Marcus?" Logan frowned, thinking, as my mind lit up like a neon sign.

"*Norman* Marcus?"

His look of consternation was replaced by a huge grin. "Yeah, that's it. You know him?"

Did I know him? He was a legend in Calgary's art world. Owned *Marcus & Bell*, the sleek gallery on 17th Avenue where everyone pretended not to want a showing. Rumour said he'd started as an architecture student who'd dropped out after a fight with his thesis advisor about "emotional geometry." He'd spent a few years in New York apprenticing under a curator at the Guggenheim, then came back in the late '80s with a Rolodex full of important names and an ego to match.

He'd been on the acquisitions board for the Glenbow Museum for five years and wrote op-eds about "the death of sincerity in postmodern expressionism." People in the art world joked that if Norman Marcus walked into your opening and didn't frown, you were halfway to making it.

"He's well-known in Calgary. At least in the art world." I tried to play it off, but my heart was beating like a humming-bird's wings. If Logan's mom had an in with him, if there was any way I could get an introduction, that would be the biggest opportunity anyone in our art department landed in years. Of course, I'd have to do something to impress him, to earn a job—or hell, even a volunteer position—but I could figure something out.

"I'd love to meet him," I blurted, already regretting all the crap I'd given Logan in the freezer aisle. But he was the one who brought it up. It wasn't like I'd pushed for him to tell me all the famous people he knew now that he was an NHL player or anything.

Logan sniffed as the employee scanned our items with a string of beeps. "I'll see what I can do."

CHAPTER
Two

WE ARRIVED on Shar's front step holding bags, with Chase still unloading from the back of the truck.

The door swung open, and Shar's eyes went wide. "What—?"

"Merry Christmas! For your immaculate conception!" Maddie teased, her breath fogging around her face.

"I did have something to do with this!" Rob called from somewhere in the back of the house.

Shar laughed. "Get in here!" She tried to move out of the way, but I had to hold the door for either of us to get past her belly.

Rob emerged from the kitchen, and when he saw us hauling bags, he dropped the dish towel he was holding and walked to the front to get his shoes. He joined Chase in full pack-mule mode. Chase entered with six bags strapped to his forearms, and Rob followed with what had to be eight.

"Not competitive at all." Shar smirked, her hands resting on her stomach shelf.

Rob grunted, slipping off his shoes and following Chase to the kitchen.

Shar grabbed a bowl of clementines from the table and

offered us one, then plunked into a chair while the guys unloaded. "This is really kind of you."

Maddie and I sat on the couch beside her, peeling our oranges.

"We hope it helps," Maddie said.

My pulse sped, my body anticipating what I had to say next. I worked on my orange and ate a slice, the sweet tang bursting in my mouth. It gave me the courage I needed. "It wasn't just us at the store."

"Oh?" Shar cocked her head to the side.

"Yeah, Logan paid for a big chunk of it." I spit the words out like I hoped she wouldn't catch his name. He'd paid for more than fifty percent, considering the diapers accounted for more than half our bill. I really hoped, for Rob and Shar's sake, that his predicted usage numbers were off.

Sharla opened her mouth, then closed it. After a moment, she said, "You saw Logan?"

I nodded. "He heard you were expecting. I actually saw him outside Ranchman's the night of your shower." Now she and Maddie were both staring at me. "He didn't want to go in, but asked if I could tell him when you were close to your due date so he could get something."

I didn't tell her how he still remembered her favourite foods or what he said about their relationship. I couldn't see how any of that would be helpful, but it made my heart twinge. Shar, Maddie, and I told each other everything. *Didn't we?*

Shar breathed for a second, then adjusted in the chair. "Wow, that's—I'm not sure what to say."

"You talking about Logan?" Rob re-entered the living room.

Shar tipped her head. "You knew about this?"

Rob shook his head. "Not that he was doing something, but I talked with him after he got back in town. He seems good."

Shar pursed her lips, her brows pinching. "That's good. It's great, actually. I don't know why I'm being weird."

Rob took up residence behind her chair and leaned over,

rubbing her shoulders. I watched the show like it was on Canadian Public Broadcasting. *And this is a modern couple. The male attempts to bring comfort to his mate while she incubates his young.*

That's how out of reach a relationship like this felt to my subconscious, apparently. I needed to create a documentary to understand it.

"Want me to kick his ass?" Rob asked.

Sharla laughed, wrapping her hands over his. "I'm not still mad—"

"It'd be fun. For old time's sake."

I'd heard about Rob and Logan's "conversation" in the Outlaw's locker room before Logan showed up and apologized to Shar. Less words, definitely more bruises.

"No, I better not. What if we want Logan to get us tickets to a game this season," Rob teased.

Maddie laughed. "The whole team?"

"Why the hell not? We do it for friends of the Hitmen." Chase squeezed in on the couch next to Maddie. And there I was again. Hugging the arm of the couch in the presence of two very in-love couples.

I pushed up. "Well, I should probably go. I've got a project to finish." Lies. But I couldn't exactly say, "I've become acutely aware of how unloved I am, and it's making me sad." Sometimes, white lies were necessary for all parties involved.

"You're not walking, we'll drive you home," Maddie said, rising. She turned to Shar as I rounded the coffee table. "Have you landed on a baby name yet?"

Shar's entire face lit. "We have a front-runner."

Maddie leaned in. "Oh?"

"Carter." Shar beamed up at Rob.

I rolled the word in my mouth like candy. "He'll definitely be hot."

Sharla chortled. "My only goal in life."

Chase shook his head. "You want him to be ugly. So he has to try harder."

Maddie laughed. "Because you're such a slacker."

"Ooh!" Sharla's hands shot out. "He's kicking. Come here!" She motioned at both of us. I dropped my shoe and ran back to the chair, falling to my knees. Shar grabbed my wrist, then Maddie's, and placed both our hands next to each other on the side of her stomach.

For a heartbeat, there was just warmth. Then, like a fish turning quickly under water, something shifted beneath my palms. I gasped. I'd felt this before, but somehow it never got less magical.

The kick pulsed again, and I laughed. "He's feisty."

"Wonder where he gets it." Maddie's eyes grew glassy.

Shar grinned. "You're stuck with him. Aunties for life."

I felt for another kick, then rose from the floor. "More like you're stuck with us. I'm going to spoil the hell out of him." Small caveat: if I got a job and wasn't still paying off student debt. Then all the toys and adorable baby clothes would be purchased.

I thought back to Logan's mention of Norman Marcus in the grocery store, and my stomach did a little flip. How well did Logan's mom know him? Would Logan actually follow through? I could already tell that waiting the next few days was going to be torturous. *And what if he never called?* I'd just have to live with that unknown for the rest of my life?

"Just trying to run out of here, eh?" Maddie stood beside me. *When had she walked over?*

"Just tired I guess." I flashed a smile and put on my shoes. She followed suit, and Chase joined us by the door.

"Thank you so much, you guys." Shar got up to see us out. Rob kept his arm looped protectively over her shoulders, and I got a flash of an image. A painting, or sculpture? A modern pregnant woman in cute maternity clothes, looking down at her belly with a caveman or Greek warrior or something curled around her, his club or sword drawn.

Huh. I'd write that down in my notebook. Not sure I had the skills to pull it off, but it had potential.

We said our goodbyes, and then we were back in the cold.

"I'm not ready for winter," Maddie groaned.

Chase pulled her close. "Vancouver's looking really good right about now." Maddie smacked him, rolling her eyes.

"What are you up to this Friday? Want to do trivia?" I asked, mostly talking to Maddie. Chase sometimes had games on the weekend, depending on the schedule.

Maddie winced. "I'm actually going to the Outlaws tournament. We leave Friday afternoon."

"Oh, I didn't realize you were still helping with that." Something twinged beneath my ribs. Maddie had been integral to the team last season, but since she started the Elite League, I assumed that was done. It was tangible proof of how little we'd talked over the past few weeks. "No worries, we can do it another time."

"I'd really love to." Maddie pulled away from Chase to give me a hug, then shoved her hands in her coat pockets and made a beeline for his truck.

I ran after her, and the truck door's metal bit in my palm, the seat's vinyl frigid as I slid in. I warmed my hands between my thighs as Chase started the engine. Yeah, I wouldn't have survived walking. They would've found me in ten minutes, standing stock still on the sidewalk. A frozen popsicle.

When I did get a car next spring, I was going to need a wheel cover. Or driving gloves, but that felt a bit pretentious. There had to be a way to improve car heating. A seat warmer? Wheel warmer? Maybe it already existed, and my family just couldn't afford it.

We pulled away from the curb, and Maddie hit the front defrost so the windshield wouldn't fog. It was only a four-minute drive, and the heat never fully kicked in, but I would never in a hundred years complain.

I hugged Maddie and thanked them both, then jogged up the

walk. Warm light filtered out of the front two windows of our fourplex. Jenna's Christmas cactus on the sill was starting to show little pink buds.

I pushed through the door, slamming it behind me so no hot air would get out.

"Hey!" Jenna called from the couch, where the latest episode of Survivor was playing. We'd all gotten really into it last season, but this time, I needed to wait until at least half the people were cut before I got invested.

The living room smelled faintly of nail polish remover and popcorn. Lindsey hunched at the table, textbooks open, high-lighter caps scattered like candy.

We were friends, the three of us. Good ones. We shared rent, rides, grocery and cooking duties. They were great. But our friendship didn't feel the same as when I was with Maddie and Shar. Here I could joke around, laugh, and problem-solve. But with them I let out my doubts, my fears. I cried with Maddie and Shar. Said the things I'd never admit to anyone else. I fit in with my roommates, but with Maddie and Shar, I belonged.

Or used to.

My mood soured a little as I dropped my things in my room. It wasn't that I couldn't say the things I used to, but it didn't feel the same. They didn't care as much about the campus or team drama, and my problems next to Shar's, bringing a literal human into the world, felt petty.

Oh, your body is growing an entirely new body? Well, I had bad period cramps yesterday. Just didn't hit the way it used to.

I dropped onto the bed, staring at the wall. My favourite painting hung next to the bed, the abstract one with the bleeding maroons and mustard-gold planes and a black line that cut through the middle. It meant one thing when I painted it. Now it looked different every time I stared at it. Today, the black line felt less like a road, more like a crack.

I shifted, and the mattress springs creaked. The whorls of my fingers were still sticky from the clementine. I rubbed them together and the scent rose again, bright and sweet. The calendar pinned to my corkboard stared at me, the white, empty spaces for this weekend yawning wide open.

My parents would be home, no doubt already curating December. My mom planning the cookie plates, my dad drawing diagrams of Christmas lights and pulling all the boxes out from the attic. I could go for the weekend, sit at the kitchen island and chat with my siblings, eat whatever casserole they were having, help with putting up the lights outside even though it was cold as balls.

The thought should've been comforting, but instead it pricked. I'd judged my brother for coming home from U of C on weekends. What kind of loser didn't have anything to do on campus?

"Hey, Crystal? There's a message for you on the machine!" Jenna called from the living room.

"Who is it?" I was comfy. I wasn't getting up to listen to some reminder that I had textbook fees due.

"I don't know, some guy?"

I shot straight up. *Had Logan called?* Had I checked the messages before I left for the grocery store? I didn't think there was anything earlier, so the message must have come during or after tonight's shopping trip.

And if it was Logan, he was quite possibly calling about Norman Marcus.

I RACED DOWN THE HALL, slowing before Jenna and Lindsey saw me so I didn't seem too desperate, then turned down the volume on the machine before pressing play.

The machine beeped. I held my breath.

"Hey, Crystal. It's Garrett."

My heart dropped, sinking into what now felt like a toxic sludge inside my middle.

"Tash is hosting a thing Saturday. You should come. We could—uh— catch up."

I hit stop. The red light stopped blinking, so I didn't need to check if there were any messages beyond that one.

Heat crawled up my neck. That night sat in my memory like a blurry Polaroid. Too much beer, Garrett heartbroken over

Maddie. I'd gone to Tash's exposition to show support, but hadn't planned on staying long. And then . . . I don't know. Kissing him felt nice. Being wanted felt nice. Until I woke up in the morning wearing his sweatshirt. We'd only made out, nothing beyond that, but it was enough to put me on Garrett's radar.

That was the extent of my dating life over the past year. Two make-out sessions, one with the guy from that Vancouver hockey team at the invitational, and Garrett. Truly an impressive showing.

"You should go," Jenna sat up on the couch to stretch. "You never go out anymore." Apparently, I hadn't turned down the volume enough.

"It's true," Lindsey said without looking up. "Your life has been boring since the summer."

I squinted at them, affection and irritation braided together. "Wow, okay. Because you two are party queens."

Lindsey sighed. "I'm an econ major. We're not supposed to have lives. Why be an art major if you can't have fun? You won't be making money."

Mm. Excellent. Roasted by my roommate, who was painting her nails the colour of alien vomit.

I picked up the receiver, the cord cool and coily against my wrist, and dialled the number from the message. The dial tone hissed, then came the quick series of beeps. Garrett answered on the second ring.

"Hello?"

"Hey, Garrett." My tone felt forced. Hopefully, he couldn't tell over the phone. "It's Crystal."

A beat, then that smile in his voice. "Hey, you."

I groaned internally. I was going to have to figure out a way to get out of this because I actually liked Tash. And currently, she was the only one pencilling in plans on my social calendar.

"Hey, so Saturday. I might swing by. Just at Tash's apartment?"

"Yep. Watching a Halloween movie. I'll save you a spot on the couch."

I winced. "Kay. I might have something else, but hopefully I'll see you then. Thanks for the invite."

I hung up, already feeling a little nauseous. I couldn't tell if it was from talking with Garrett or because I'd been so hopeful it would be Logan's voice sounding from the speaker.

"Very convincing," Jenna said.

I flipped her the bird as I walked back to my room.

———

On Friday morning, the studio smelled like wet plaster. Sunlight filtered through the high windows, hitting the dust motes that always danced there in the morning. Someone's Walkman hissed quietly on the table, the tinny sound of Alanis bleeding through one earpiece. I would've turned it off, but I never wanted to mess with a part of anyone's creative process.

My table looked like a battlefield: wire spools, bent pliers, a half-formed armature that could've been a bird, a broken umbrella, or a paranormal creature. I'd been here since eight and it was nearly noon. Everything I'd made reminded me of Michelangelo's half-formed carvings, except nobody was going to display my partial creations in Florence.

I twisted another length of wire, the metal biting into my thumb. I muttered a curse under my breath. This was supposed to be a piece about tension—about dichotomies and paradox— but right now it was really only about me wanting to throw things. I stepped back, squinted, tilted my head like that might help.

Nope. Still a sad coat hanger.

I scrapped it. Again.

Maybe I was just tired. Or maybe my looming graduation date with zero prospects and shitty social life was scraping out my proverbial creative bucket. I didn't want to give credence to that thought. That would mean my well of inspiration was out of my control. For an artist, that idea was more terrifying than meeting a bear in the woods.

I ran a hand through my hair and caught on a strand of hardened plaster. For one ridiculous second, I pictured myself marching to the nearest salon and asking them to shave it all off. No more pink highlights or cute curtain bangs. Just a new beginning.

It was a fun thought experiment, but I wasn't that brave, so I tied it up and grabbed more plaster strips.

Kyle strode in and picked up his Walkman, settled the headphones over his head, and picked up where he left off on his project across the room. It looked to be the size of a lawnmower. The sheer confidence was enviable.

Maybe that was all I needed. A little more *je ne c'est quoi*. A bit of hubris, less identity crisis. Wasn't that how everyone I knew landed their internships and assistant positions? I was already spinning fantasies in my head of meeting Norman Marcus if Logan followed up. What I would wear, what version of myself Norman would be interested in.

But the odds of Logan actually getting me an intro were slim to none. Especially after how I'd treated him at Co-op. Though he had brought it up at the checkout line.

No. I didn't need to get my hopes up.

I slipped my fingers over the cool plaster, removing the excess from the strip and letting it drip onto the newspaper-covered tabletop. It wasn't the end of the world. If I didn't get some magical connection, grad school was the fallback. UBC, maybe. McGill, if I got brave. Master's in Art History or Curatorial Studies. Two more years to figure this all out.

The plaster strip stiffened in my hand. I pressed it against the armature, watched it take shape. Maybe that's just what artists did. We built ourselves like we built our art. Creating something fragile, over and over again, until something finally held.

————

A half hour later, I rinsed my hands in the sink until the water ran clear, flakes of plaster circling the drain. I stacked my tools, wiped down the table, and took one last look at the half-finished sculpture. From this angle, it almost looked intentional. Almost.

Outside, the sky had dimmed to that flat grey that meant snow or rain or both. I shoved my hands into my coat pockets and headed toward the path that cut across campus. The cold bit at my nose.

"MacMillan!"

I turned to see Axel and Rory coming out of the North Centre. Both wore their Outlaws jackets, hockey bags slung over one shoulder. Behind them was another guy who was a little taller with darker hair, and—

I sucked in a breath.

It took me a second to place him since it was so out of context, but that was number twelve. Jake. From the invitational last spring. When we'd returned our cafeteria trays after sledding, and made out by the dish return slot, right between the industrial sinks.

"Hey." Recognition lit up his face. "Crystal, right?"

"Oh, hey," I said, trying to sound casual while my stomach did somersaults. Guys you made out with once on a whim weren't supposed to show up in your real life. That was the whole point of hockey tournaments.

"Wait, you two know each other?" Axel raised an eyebrow.

I scoffed. "Not really, just met at the invitational."

Jake looked smug, and my cheeks heated.

"Okay, I was surprised because he just joined the team last week."

I nearly choked on my spit. "Oh yeah?"

Rory clapped his hand on Jake's shoulder. "He was impressed by our showing in Clearwater. Decided to transfer. Coach put him through the ringer in practices, but he's official."

Jake adjusted the strap of his bag, his eyes still on me. "You all hang out?"

Rory snorted. "She's been avoiding us, bud. We used to see her all the time. Now it's like she joined witness protection."

"I've been around," I said, a bit too defensively. "Just busy."

Axel grinned. "Nah. You just love Maddie and Shar more than us."

I laughed. "I mean, you said it."

Rory pretended to be hurt. "Well, Maddie's coming to the tourney this weekend. Is that enough to get you to come?"

I blew out a breath. "Some of us have actual homework to do." I did have things I could work on, but a part of me wondered if I should call up Maddie and invite myself along. Sounded a lot better than sitting on a couch with Garrett.

"We'll have to plan something when we get back then," Axel pulled me into a hug, squeezing the air from my lungs. "Promise?"

"Fine," I grunted. "I guess."

Rory ruffled my hair and I slapped his hand away. They laughed and waved. Jake walked backward a step or two before joining them.

Have mercy. What was wrong with me? I should've been jumping all over that, but the idea of hanging out with the team filled me with dread instead of excitement. It just wasn't the same.

By the time I reached the fourplex, my fingers were numb. I dropped my bag beside the couch, kicked off my shoes, and microwaved some leftover pasta. I rinsed my bowl, wiped my hands on a dish towel, and spotted the red blink of the answering machine.

I grabbed a pen and notepad, pressing play.

There was a beep, then a low voice. "Hey, Crystal. It's Logan."

The pen froze midair.

"I wanted to check in about that gallery thing. I talked to my mom, and she said Norman's open to meeting you. If you're still interested. I think he's going to be over at the space tomorrow afternoon or evening. It's a weekend, so I get it if you have plans . . ."

No, the hell I did not have plans. Not anymore. I scrawled down the address and time on my notepad, and as soon as the message ended, I picked up the phone and dialled Logan back.

Funny, I didn't have to check my notebook. I had his number memorized.

CHAPTER
Four

THE PHONE RANG TWICE.

"Hello?" Logan's voice sounded rough, like I'd woken him up.

I glanced at the clock over the microwave. Must be nice. "Were you sleeping?"

Logan yawned. "No."

"Sounds like you were sleeping."

"Well, I'm not now."

I twirled the phone cord on my finger and leaned against the wall. "Is this your life? You make six figures while sleeping past noon?"

"I didn't realize I was talking to my mom."

I rolled my eyes even though he couldn't see it. "I'm just jealous." I could've slept in if I wanted, but my head was too full to stay in bed. "It's Crystal, by the way."

"Yeah. I know."

My heart sped up. It was weird talking to him one-on-one like this. "I got your message."

"Oh. I thought you were just calling for fun." A smirk was audible in his voice, and I squeezed my eyes closed to erase the mental image of him lying shirtless in bed.

"Nope." It took me a minute to remember why I called in the first place. "So, Saturday."

"Yeah."

I slid down the wall and sat on the floor in the doorway to the kitchen. "Are you serious that I'm invited to meet Norman Marcus?"

"Why do you keep saying that like he's a god or something?"

"Because he is."

Logan chuckled. "I didn't know you were into sixty-year-olds."

"Well, there's a lot you don't know about me. And he's a total silver fox."

"So is my dad. Are you into him, too?"

I laughed. "Depends. Does he own art galleries?"

From the rustle through the speaker, I gathered Logan was shifting on the bed. He grunted. "Not that I know of."

"How did your dad become friends with Norman Marcus?"

"Just call him Norman."

"No."

"It's weird that you keep saying his full name."

I kicked my feet up on the opposite side of the doorframe. "Deal with it."

Logan blew out a breath. "It's my mom."

"What?"

"My mom is friends with him, not my dad. She's an artist."

My mouth dropped open. *Logan's mom was an artist?* How had that never come up before? "What's her medium?"

"She paints, but it's over this rough surface, kind of scuffed and destroyed. I don't know how to describe it."

I had a thousand questions. "Does she sell it? Or display it anywhere?"

"She sells to galleries, yeah. They're in a few places in town."

WHAT. Shar was going to get a talking to. She could've at least mentioned this before everything went down last winter. "That's incredible. I'd love to see it."

"Serious?"

"Yes, I'm being serious." I shouldn't have sounded so shocked. It was a fair question, considering I'd given him ninety percent sarcasm in all of our in-person conversations up to that point. But that was before he started speaking my language.

He blew out a breath against the phone receiver. "Okay."

We both paused, and my heart got nervous and jumpy at the sudden silence. "So if your mom knows Norman *Marcus*—" I left in the last name just to mess with him, "how are you not giving him the respect he deserves? You must know who he is, and yet you want to call him buddy Norm—"

"I don't really know who he is."

I made a noise that was half gasp, half scoff. "Logan, he's *the* guy. Norman Marcus has been consulting for the Glenbow since before we could walk. The man once petitioned for the National Gallery to feature a canola field painted by a man who was legally blind. People quote his critiques like scripture. My first year at Douglas, I skipped a midterm review to watch him speak at the Rozsa. He's—" Even without seeing Logan's face, I could tell I was losing him. I needed to make this more relevant. "He's the Pavel Bure of the art world. Everyone's copying his moves and pretending they came up with them first."

Silence. Then an "Oh, Shit," from Logan.

"Yeah."

"So this is a big deal."

"Correct." I pinched the bridge of my nose. Maybe that was the key to life, never understanding the weight of your actions. "Ignorance is bliss" and all that. Here Logan was, casually setting up breakfast with the man who curated *Bodies Held*. Provocative rebar torsos hanging from steel cables. I wrote an entire paper on it. That show rewired my brain.

"He just seems like a normal guy. He's been around since I was in high school," he went on. "My parents host these dinners. Charity and art events. I just thought he was rich."

I laughed. "Well, he is that. Has he ever shown your mom's work?"

"Yep. A couple of times. She has this new series she's doing. I think he's going to feature it in the new space."

Hope fizzed in my chest. This was the opportunity of a lifetime. To have an in? To be able to meet Mr. Marcus through an artist he already appreciated?

Impostor syndrome immediately set in. What would I even say to him? Would I have anything to offer besides sweat equity?

I shifted on the floor. My left leg was going numb. "He's not going to take me seriously."

"Join the club."

"What does that mean?"

Logan sighed. "Nothing."

"Doesn't sound like nothing." I held my breath, wondering if he'd open up. Then chastised myself when I realized how much I wanted him to.

This was Logan. Selfish, egotistical, Logan. But as much as I tried to activate the anger I'd felt in the grocery store, I could barely get it to spark. He was doing something nice for me. For no reason. At least . . . not that I could see.

"So, what do you even bring to something like this? Do you show up with a briefcase or something?" Logan asked.

I snorted. "Do I seem like a briefcase person to you?"

"I don't know," he said. "What does a briefcase person look like?"

"Like Maddie."

He barked a laugh. "Yeah. Fair."

"I'll bring slides," I said, warming up now. "Photos, my sculpture pieces, maybe a one-page artist statement."

"What's that?"

"It's like when reporters ask what kind of player you are and you say 'I'm a team player, I trust all these guys.'"

Logan laughed out loud. "You watched that interview?"

"It wasn't an option *not* to watch it. It was playing on every TV on campus."

He sighed. "I meant what I said."

"No you didn't! You aren't a team player, you want to bury the puck."

"Maybe I'm not the same person I was last year."

"Uh, maybe you are." I wasn't going to admit I'd watched one of his preseason games. It just happened to be on one night when I had the flu from hell. It was stranger than fiction to hear the commentators saying his name.

His laugh came back softer. "People can change, Crys. Uh, Crystal. Sorry. I didn't—"

"My brother calls me Crys."

There was another rustle of fabric against the speaker. "Do you like your brother?"

Was he joking? I waited for a chuckle but it didn't come. The question made me pause. Had I ever considered whether I *liked* my siblings? "I think so."

"You think?"

I launched into an explanation of how my brother always messed with me growing up. There were plenty of times I hadn't liked him, and he was still able to get under my skin with barely a look, but all of that was kind of exactly why I liked him. We had all that history together. There was nobody else on earth who knew me like him.

Logan told me about the cousin he grew up with, the closest thing he had to a brother besides his hockey teammates. How he still felt like Rob was family, even though they barely talked anymore.

That reminded me of a spat with my sister, which then took me into a diatribe about my dad's workshop, the place that sparked my love of art. I had just scooched onto the edge of the carpet and flipped onto my stomach, propping my head on my free hand, when Jenna's feet appeared in front of my nose.

I craned my neck to look up.

Her arms were crossed. "You've been on the phone for an hour."

My brows pinched. "What?" Wait, when had she gotten home? I didn't even hear the front door open and shut. I held the receiver to my shoulder. "Were you in your room?"

"No, I came in fifteen minutes ago."

"Then how do you—"

"Because I tried to phone you from campus. They were giving out free pizza in the quad."

I considered making some argument about how this was a second phone call, but thought better of it.

I flipped the phone back into place against my ear. "Hey, I have to go. My roommate needs the phone."

"Oh, yeah. Sure. See you tomorrow."

I scrambled up from the floor. "Wait, give me the details again."

He rattled off the time and address, and I scrawled them on the notepad.

Logan waited, then asked, "How is everyone?"

"Uh, you mean the team?"

"Yeah. Or whoever. You know, just people at Douglas."

I set the pen down on the counter. Did he sound a bit defensive? "I think everyone's good."

"Again with the thinking."

I laughed. "I don't see people as much as I did last year. You know, with Maddie and Chase and Shar and Rob—" I cut myself off, realizing I'd treaded into awkward territory. "You know how it is. They're doing their thing."

Logan grunted again. "Team's doing well, at least."

"Only a couple of games in. First tourney games are tomorrow." I thought back to Rory, Axel, and Jake. Maybe I should put more effort into those relationships. I thought Jake was only a fling, but if he was here? If I could get something going, and he got along with my friends? Then I wouldn't be a fifth wheel. We could actually triple date and—

"Crystal!" Jenna made an exasperated noise.

"Right. Okay, sorry, I've got to go." We said our goodbyes, and when the dial tone buzzed in my ear, I clicked the phone back into place on the wall mount. I expected Jenna to swoop in and grab it, but instead, she still stood a few feet away, watching me.

"What?" I asked, not loving the smug look on her face.

"Who is he?"

"Uhhhh, just a friend." By the triumphant gleam in her eye, I knew I'd hesitated too long.

"You said 'your roommate.'"

"So?"

Her smirk curled at the edges. "Any *friend* would know your roommates' names. He's new."

I rolled my eyes and walked past her into the living room. "I make new friends all the time."

"Not men! Who you talk to for an hour!" she called after me as I hustled into my room and shut the door behind me.

In hindsight, running away with my tail between my legs was probably not the best way to prove my innocence.

I flopped onto the bed and turned my alarm clock toward me. Had it really been an hour? The whole conversation had felt like five minutes.

I closed my eyes and blew out a breath. If I talked with Logan for an hour, I clearly wasn't getting enough socialization. My stomach grumbled, making me regret that conversation for more than one reason. There was never a good excuse to miss free pizza.

BUT.

Tomorrow I was going to meet Norman Marcus.

I grinned at the ceiling. Logan shouldn't have made a big deal out of it. When he was around, I was eternally bound to speak Norman's full name.

CHAPTER
Five

NO SURPRISE, but I couldn't sleep that night. I put together a small art portfolio on my floor at three in the morning. A much more productive option than lying on the couch and watching Sex in the City for three hours.

Prints and slides fanned out over the rug like an archaeological dig of my brain. Wire-and-plaster pieces from Sculpture II. A few charcoal studies. The mixed-media canvases.

Thankfully, I'd borrowed a portfolio case from the studio a couple of weeks ago when I took a few paintings to my parents. I'd berated myself for not returning it yet, but now it was coming in handy. I swapped out one photo for another, then swapped it back. It really wasn't a life-or-death situation. I wanted a job, not representation.

Jenna stuck her head in around eight. I'd filled her in on the opportunity last night after coming up with a story to explain my lengthy phone chat. It was networking, that was all. I left Logan's name completely out of it.

"Need a ride?"

"I'm borrowing Rob's truck." He was gone for the weekend at the tournament and always left a spare set of keys out for me. "Thanks for the offer, though."

She nodded. "Tell me how it goes."

"You know where I live."

She snorted and retreated to the living room. I probably needed to make more effort with my roommates, too. They were kind enough to still give me the time of day even though I blew them off to be attached to Maddie and Shar's hips the last couple of years.

Which reminded me . . . Tash. She would probably kill for an opportunity like this. I chewed on my lower lip. It wasn't my invitation to make, but if it went well and something came of this meeting, then I could find a way to introduce her. Right? It was the best I could do at the moment.

I put on my coat and slung the case over my shoulder. Outside, Calgary had that early-winter blue where the cold punched straight through you, making you cough. Frost rimmed the fourplex steps, and my breath plumed in clouds as I half-walked, half-jogged the twenty minutes to Rob and Sharla's.

I finagled the keys out from the wheel well, and the truck started up without much complaint. I'd printed out a map at some point during the night, and the directions weren't hard. Still, my nerves did the wave during red lights.

Hi, I'm Crystal. Thank you for meeting me. Too formal.

Norman— too familiar.

Mr. Marcus, it's an honour— too grovelly.

By the time I hit 17th Avenue, I'd landed on flattery. Full and complete butt kissing. That's what he was surely used to.

Downtown rose up in front of me, all glass and steel with the Bow doing its quiet loop-the-loop under bridges. The sky was the colour of pencil shavings. Even with the heat on, I could smell snow coming. It always smelled like cow manure when a storm was blowing in.

Logan told me to meet at a warehouse near the turnoff to Stampede Park, down a side street with loading docks and dumpsters. A little murder-y, but I turned in, parked, and killed the engine.

That's when I saw him.

Logan was leaning against the brick near an unmarked metal door, hands in the pockets of a charcoal coat, hair damp. With his fogging breath, he looked like he was posing for a magazine shoot.

I was the teensiest bit curious about him. About what he looked like under his clothes. Up close. Sure, I'd seen him strip off his shirt now and then, but I wasn't *looking*. Shar always used to talk about his abs or his shoulders. It wasn't his appearance that soured the relationship. That was for damn sure.

I shook my head and pulled out the keys. He straightened when he clocked the truck. Rob's truck. It hit him, and he flinched just a little, his shoulders lifting and dropping, his hands shoving deeper into his pockets.

I would've felt a little guilty for bringing it, but Logan didn't once mention that he'd be meeting me here. I thought I was showing up for a meeting with Norman Marcus solo, which was terrifying. If Logan had said he was coming, I might've been able to get some shut-eye.

I climbed out, portfolio banging the door on the way. "What the hell?"

"Good morning to you, too."

I locked the door. "You didn't say you were coming."

Logan strode toward me with lazy steps. "You thought I'd make you come here by yourself?" He motioned to the dirty alley.

"Well, it is before noon."

He scoffed. "Once again. Didn't know I was that big of a dick."

I stopped in front of him. "This self-deprecating thing isn't a good look."

Logan's expression hardened. "It's a good thing I don't have to rely on my sense of humour then."

Heat flashed in my middle. The fact that he was pulling me a solid at the moment flew out the window. "Hm. Still a big hit with the ladies?"

He wet his lips and nodded. "All they need to hear is NHL."

"Nice." I stalked past him before I could say something else I'd regret later. I didn't need to get into this with him. Obviously, he hadn't learned much from everything that happened, or maybe he realized he didn't want a serious relationship. That was an improvement, wasn't it? Still, the way he said it. Logan was excellent at pressing my rage button.

He jogged to catch up. "I was kidding."

"Yeah, okay."

"I'm not—I don't sleep around."

I shrugged, slowing when he edged in front of me. "You can do whatever you want. It's not like I'm dating you."

Logan watched me for a moment, and my heart picked up speed. Right as I was about to say something to break the silence, he nodded toward the door. "My mom's already inside."

I smirked, then continued on my path.

"What's that look supposed to mean?"

"It was just a smile."

Logan easily caught up with his long strides. "It was a judgy smile."

"Not judgy. Just funny to think that you woke up because your mom told you to." I reached for the door handle, but Logan's wingspan doubled mine. Even from two steps behind me, he snatched it first.

I gave him a look. "Really? Chivalry?"

He did a little shrug, like maybe he didn't want a gold star. "Can't win with you."

"Are you trying to?" I teased, but Logan didn't laugh.

"Maybe."

My stomach flipped like I'd just been double-bounced on the trampoline. I gripped the portfolio strap a little tighter. *Maybe?* What the hell did that mean? I really needed to kiss Jake or someone, preferably not Garrett again, because my body was clearly getting a little desperate.

We walked into a long, newly drywalled hall lit by end-of-day sunlight drifting through the dirty windows. "Can I ask something?"

"Shoot."

"Why are you doing this for me?"

He rubbed the back of his neck. "Honestly?"

"If you're capable of telling the truth."

That time, he huffed a laugh. As we walked a few more steps, his smile slipped a little. "When Shar broke up with me, I went into a whole . . . thing. Six months of trying to figure out what was wrong with me. Then I . . . " His cheeks coloured.

"What?"

He shook his head. "It's embarrassing."

"Well, now you have to tell me." I couldn't get a bead on him. One minute he was making jokes about hooking up with puck bunnies, and the next, saying he was doing deep introspective work?

Logan dragged his feet, and he looked suddenly boyish. My awareness of how much he'd changed since I saw him last snapped forward. He had full stubble on his jaw, not just patches like before. His face was leaner, like he'd lost the last of his baby fat. He looked like a man, and that was . . . well, kind of a huge turn on.

I blinked and locked my eyes straight ahead, giving myself an internal lecture. *Muscles good, muscles on Logan, bad.*

He lowered his voice. "I called my other exes."

My head whipped back toward him. "You, what?"

He nodded. "I know. Crazy. But after everything Rob said—"

"What did Rob say?" I couldn't hide my curiosity. Shar told us that Rob had suggested Logan talk to her before she moved out, but everything we heard from the guys told a slightly different story. Involving dropped gloves and bloody noses.

"I don't know if I should—"

"Logan!" A woman with a classy, blond bob appeared through a doorway across the open warehouse space. Her heels clicked against the concrete floor. "For goodness' sake, what took you so long?"

Wow. That had to be Logan's mom, and it turned out she was super hot. She looked completely out of place in her pencil skirt and light pink blouse against the mess and construction. The concrete floors were dusted with saw grit. Scaffolding lined the walls where they were installing specialty light fixtures, and worklights threw yellow pools across taped-off rectangles on the floor. And here she was, all shiny and fresh. She probably smelled like Yves St. Lauren. My foolproof rubric for judging someone's level of wealth.

"Sorry." Logan smiled and pulled her into a bear hug. "Just catching up."

She pushed back and adjusted her hair, then gave him a look that said *"get the hell in there, you're late"* before turning her attention on me. "You must be Crystal?"

I nodded, feeling very underdressed in my jeans and sweater. *But they were my nice jeans.* I put out a hand and shook hers in greeting.

She looked me up and down. "I'm Alice. Come on. We don't want to keep Norman waiting."

Logan flashed a smirk, and I knew exactly what he was thinking. *See? That's how you say his name like a normal person.* I swallowed my snarky reply, not wanting his mom to overhear it. But it would've been a good one.

We walked into a makeshift office with cloudy tarps as walls. Norman Marcus stood at a long table covered in drawings and coffee cups. Black turtleneck, silver glasses, salt-and-pepper hair that curled neatly at the collar. He looked like the kind of person who could stare a painting into hanging straighter.

Nobody spoke, and it took him a moment to look up. He seemed deep in thought, scrutinizing something on a piece of paper, one hand planted on the desk, the other lifted to his mouth where one finger tapped his lower lip thoughtfully.

I mean, who wouldn't be into this guy, age be damned.

Norman inhaled, snapping out of whatever thought he'd been living in, and straightened. He clicked his tongue. "Ah. You're here." He had the faintest French accent, and that only added to the mystique.

"Hello." I gave a small wave, managing not to call him Sir or Your Majesty, which took real effort. He rounded the desk, and I shook his hand—*I, Crystal MacMillan shook Norman Marcus's hand.*

"Coffee?" Alice asked, striding toward a side table with a coffee maker plugged into an orange extension cord.

"Please," I said, right as Logan said, "I can get it."

Alice waved him off. "Do your introduction, it's fine."

Logan nodded. "Right. So, this is—"

"Crystal," Norman finished, his eyes travelling to the portfolio bag. "You're in your final year at Douglas, yes?" I nodded.

Norman gestured to the area outside the tent. "We're building a hybrid space. A working artist studio plus exhibition hall. I want it to be a living, breathing thing. Where art can inspire retroactively, one continuous round."

My mouth was hanging open. I quickly closed it.

Alice handed me a steaming cup of coffee, but didn't pass Logan his. "May I have a moment?" She smiled sweetly, tipping her head toward the door. Well, tent slit.

Logan looked between the two of us, but I cut his discomfort out at the knees. "It's fine. I'm good."

His lips parted like he was going to say something, but his mom was already walking. He turned and followed, and I had *so* many questions.

Logan's life was picture-perfect. His parents paid for him to attend premier hockey camps. He never had to work a job in high school, his university was completely covered, and his dad paid for the townhouse he lived in. Now, not only was his dad a real-estate mogul, but his mom seemed to be a total ball-buster.

I loved my family, but what would it have been like to grow up like that?

"May I see?" Norman asked, pointing to my bag, and I thought my heart might explode out of my chest.

All of the art pieces I'd brought flashed in my head, and none of them were good enough. Not to show *him*. The idea of spinning and running back to the parking lot seemed far more attractive than walking toward the desk, but Logan wasn't fully out of the tent yet. He was blocking my exit.

I stepped forward and slipped the strap off my shoulder, laying the bag flat while trying not to mess up the papers and file folders he had sitting there. "These are just a few samples. I've been exploring different mediums this year."

I was going to die. Norman Marcus asked to look at my art pieces. What if he hated them? Worse, what if he was indifferent? Would I have to quit everything and switch my major to communications?

"As you should." Norman watched me unzip and unfold the bag. Before I could say anything else, he reached in and began examining.

My palms were damp enough, I had to wipe them on my coat. Norman studied in silence. The murmur of Alice's voice sounded from outside the tent.

"Wire and plaster," Norman commented, finally. "I like that you make them fight."

"They started fighting without me," I said, and he let out an amused "hm."

He leaned back and turned a photo sideways, then straight. "And colour?"

"Less." It was my immediate answer. I wasn't even sure what he was asking, but it felt right. I'd found that I was using little to none at all in everything outside of painting. Even then, I was muting the pigments.

He thumbed through my next pieces and paused on a charcoal sketch. "This is unresolved."

"That's the point."

He looked up. "What do you hate in contemporary shows?"

I blinked. "Hate?"

"Yes." His face was all patience.

This was by far the weirdest job interview I'd ever had. "I would have to say . . . I hate when galleries treat the audience like they have to feel something. Or the same thing, I guess. Like there's one right answer."

His expression remained impassive. "And what do you love?"

That one was easier. "When the space makes a conversation happen. When a piece yanks a line out of another piece across the room and you don't know why until your stomach tells your head to catch up."

He was silent a moment, then he lifted the piece in his hand. "This goes in the opening."

My heart stalled. "I—what?"

"Opening," he repeated, like he understood my short-circuiting brain. "We'll show one of yours alongside three established artists. I'll want process photos and a short statement." His eyes scanned my portfolio again, then lifted to mine. "But tell me, do you want to be *shown* or *involved*?"

My mouth answered before my anxiety could think. "Involved," I said. "I love making, but curation is—" I groped for an explanation, "My end game. I want to help people discover."

His eyes narrowed. "I wasn't talking about curation."

"Oh, I know, I was just saying that eventually—"

"Good taste and the ability to express oneself to collectors must be honed over time."

I nodded, practically swallowing my tongue. "Of course." My eyes dropped, my cheeks flaming. Why had I said that? Of course he wasn't going to offer me a job when we'd barely just met.

"But I do need help with outreach. Organization and exhibit prep."

My head shot up, and I blurted, "Yes," before I could think. "I'll do all of it—or any of it, I should say. I'd be honoured."

The corner of Norman's mouth twitched. "Perfect." He strode back to stand behind the desk and pulled something from the top drawer. "Pay is nine dollars an hour."

My eyes widened. That was two dollars per hour more than what I ever made working on campus.

"Hours will be flexible. You can prioritize school as needed, but I will expect a certain level of commitment."

"Of course."

He smiled, writing something on the papers in front of him. "It will be a win-win, really."

I forced my lungs to fill. "I would hope so."

Norman paused his writing. "I can't have a historic display without paying homage to Canada's love affair with hockey, and having you here will only mean good press."

My giddiness morphed into confusion. Hockey? And me? How were those two things going to garner publicity?

I tried not to panic, searching for any explanation that made sense. I did go to hockey games. The Outlaws had gone to nationals, but what did that have to do with Norman's gallery?

"I'm not quite sure what you mean." After giving Logan crap about honesty, I decided to take my own advice and ask.

Norman looked up, his pen still pressed to paper. "Oh, don't tell me you don't have Logan wrapped around your little finger."

Before shock could register on my face, Norman spun the paper to face me. "I've written in a few mandatory events and press opportunities. If you can make sure your boyfriend attends, and preferably a few of his teammates as well, the job is yours."

My stomach crashed to the floor. My boyfriend? *Shit.* Norman Marcus thought Logan and I were dating. Was that the only reason he met with me today? He was doing some kind of sports exhibit and needed outreach and press?

Of course. Why wouldn't he want to secure support from the Blizzard, but Logan was already here, wasn't he? His mom was a family friend. She was being featured in the show, so why wouldn't that be enough to nail him down?

I stared at the signature line on the contract. Mandatory events. Press opportunities. Make sure your boyfriend attends. *I couldn't speak for him, could I?* Or did Logan know this was the deal? Had he forgotten to tell me that Norman thought we were an item?

Norman blew out a breath and glanced at his watch. "I've got to run. If you need time to think about it—"

"No." I stepped forward, picking up the pen. My chest felt like a balloon about to pop. We would just figure this out. I'd tell Logan about this craziness and we'd laugh and then he'd explain to Marcus that we weren't actually together—

But then why would Norman need me?

Blood rushed in my ears as I signed on the dotted line. This was wrong. I shouldn't be pretending I was with Logan. I shouldn't be pretending I could commit to the dates Norman had written in.

But this might be my only chance. My only in.

As soon as I lifted the pen, Norman pulled the contract from the table top, then handed me a blank one. "For your reference. Hours start Monday if you're available."

CHAPTER
Six

AFTER ANOTHER FITFUL SLEEP, I stared at the contract copy Norman had given me. The apartment was quiet. Lindsey was already at work, and Jenna was doing something at the cosmetology school. She'd finished her hours, but she was doing some kind of extra certification. Maddie was still in Lethbridge with the guys, and Shar was in baby-land.

Today, it was just me and my lies. Mismatched socks, crooked hair clip, no good food in the fridge. It was what a dishonest, self-absorbed, corporate ladder climber deserved.

I stared at the dates until my eyes burned, then dragged my sorry butt out of bed and forced myself into the kitchen to at least find crackers and peanut butter. The idea of going to the grocery store only made me think of Logan, which catalyzed my shame spiral all over again.

Why did I sign it? Why didn't I take a minute to at least talk with Logan?

I knew the answer, of course, but it wasn't comforting. I was such a hypocrite. What had I said? Something about him being incapable of honesty? That was rich.

He was never going to let me hear the end of this. I had to tell him. There was no getting around that. And then he'd hold my potential career in his egotistical hands.

I pulled out a sleeve of Ritz and opened the jar of Kraft peanut butter, grabbing a knife. I might be a two-faced ambition junkie, but I wasn't a dip-straight-from-the-jar kind of heathen.

I ate in silence until the crunch of my own teeth was too much to take, and snagged the phone from the wall. I needed to talk to someone, and since it couldn't be Maddie or Shar, that left one option.

I dialled Tash's number. No answer.

It was ten-thirty, which meant she was probably still sleeping. But she'd likely be up soon. I debated, but I didn't take long to make a decision. In less than five minutes, I'd put away my squirrel snack and pulled on boots and a scarf.

Since Maddie moved out, Tash didn't renew her lease. She was now living three blocks over with different roommates. Friends of Garrett's. It was very convenient for my current predicament, even though I did technically still have Rob's truck.

Tash opened the door in plaid PJ pants, her bra, and smudged eyeliner that made a perfect smoky eye. I'd expect nothing less.

"Oh, good," she mumbled. "Just who I was hoping to see."

I followed her in without an invitation. "Good morning, sunshine."

"Don't good morning me. You ditched us last night." She flopped onto the couch and burritoed in a blanket. "I had a movie and questionable men queued up."

"Garrett and his friends don't count as questionable." I dropped into the armchair. "I'm really sorry, by the way. Turns out, it was a terrible life choice."

Her ears perked up. "Tell me more."

"Hm, where to start? I met Norman Marcus and—"

"Shut up!"

"I know. I wasn't sure how it was going to go, but it went

really well until I found out that the only reason I was there was that he thought I was dating Logan Kemp."

Tash leaned in. "Wait. NHL player Logan Kemp? Wasn't he dating your friend, Shar until that picture in the paper came out?"

I nodded. Yes to all of the above. "Norman thought we were together."

Her brows shot up. "I'm sorry?"

I let out a groan. "He offered me a job, but it requires us—me and Logan—to show up at different events. As boyfriend and girlfriend."

Tash's mind was working. "Why the hell would Norman Marcus care who you're dating?"

I threw out my arms. "Right? He's opening this new gallery, an artist collective space, and doing some kind of historical feature involving hockey. He's convinced that I, as Logan's significant other, can convince him to show up for the press."

Realization dawned on Tash's face. "Oh. Because he plays for the Blizzard."

"Exactly."

Tash chewed on this for a moment. "I don't see the problem."

I pressed my fingers against my temples. "Of course you don't."

"No, I'm serious. When does the gallery open?"

My mouth opened and closed like a fish. That would've been a good question to ask.

"Okay, you don't know. That's fine. But it can't be too long if he's already thinking about promotion."

"So?"

"So, you tell Logan you want to do it until the opening, then you part ways amicably, or have a dramatic public breakup, whichever you prefer, and voila."

"Voila? I see no 'voila!' This is Logan Kemp, Tash. Shar's ex. There's no way I can commit to spending so much time with him —I don't want to spend that much time with him. And I don't want people to think we're dating, plus the fact that I don't want to start off this job—a potential stepping stone to future incredible opportunities, on a lie!"

Tash laughed out loud. "What, you think everyone in the arts just made it there because of their talent? Do you know how many lies manager moms tell about their kids to get them acting gigs? They make up false addresses, birth certificates—"

"Yeah, okay, I get it, but I don't want that to be me! Why should I have to link myself to some guy to get ahead?"

She gave me a look. "Babe."

"Babe."

Tash let out a slow breath. "You're literally preaching to the choir, but that system isn't changing anytime soon. We can sit here and bitch about it, or we can use it to our advantage." She reached for her glass on the end table and took a very sketchy sideways drink of some liquid that wasn't quite clear. "What have you got to lose?"

That question gave me pause. The job. I had the job to lose. But would I lose it if Norman found out I wasn't actually dating Logan . . . or would I lose it faster by telling the truth?

I thought back to that plastic room. How eager he'd been, how fast he'd wanted me to sign.

"Okay." I sucked in a breath and held it. "Okay."

"There you go."

I leaned over my knees. "So, what, I tell Logan? Hope he'll go along with it?"

She grinned. "Oh, he'll go along with it."

My face screwed up. "I don't see how that's obvious."

"Um, he went to the grocery store with you guys to buy baby food."

"Actual food, not baby food."

"Whatever. And then he shows up at this thing? Sets up a meeting?"

I still wasn't catching what she was throwing.

Tash pulled herself up to sit. "He's lonely."

I scoffed. "Logan? He's playing on the Blizzard. He has a whole team and a thousand girls throwing themselves at him."

"Yeah. So why is he at a Co-op with two of his ex's best friends? Why is he at a gallery with you instead of sleeping off a hangover?"

Both excellent questions. *I don't sleep around.*

I swallowed hard. "There's one slight problem."

"And that is?"

"I was . . . a bit self-righteous. At the store and the warehouse."

Tash smirked. "Can I please be a fly on the wall when you make this phone call?"

———

Neither of us had classes because of the government holiday, so we rewatched the last half of the movie since it didn't have to be returned to Blockbuster until tomorrow. Then we walked onto campus to get lunch from the cafeteria and returned to our couch potato status by about three o'clock in the afternoon.

After talking and laughing, we made tacos with the mystery meat Tash had in the fridge, and I finally felt prepared to face the music. I decided to phone him from her apartment because, frankly, I needed the moral support. If anything good was going to come from this, I figured it might as well be Tash's happiness.

Two rings. Four. Then a party swallowed the line.

"Hello?"

Bass thumped. Bottles clinked. I couldn't even tell if it was him until a female voice cooed, "Logan, leave it. Come back to the couch."

My stomach knotted.

"Hang on—yeah? Hello?" Logan sounded more than a little breathless.

I tried to hang up, but Tash caught my arm. "Um, yeah, it's me. Crystal." She said for me, then pressed the receiver back to my ear.

"Oh! Hey!" Something scraped against the speaker. "One sec —" Muffled shuffle. "Can you hear me? Sorry, it's loud. I had the guys over tonight, and it—Pace, shut up for a sec—hang on—"

This sounded like old Logan. Life of the party, Logan. This was the Logan I'd learned to resent the most. Because whenever he was taking shots or goofing off with the boys, Shar had been sitting off to the side. I'd never liked that dynamic, even when things were good between them.

"It's fine. You're busy. I can—"

"No, wait, it's good." The noise died away with the slam of a door. "There. What's up?"

My mind went blank now that I had his attention. "Uh, no, it's nothing. I think—I don't know, maybe it's better if I phone tom—"

"Is this about the contract?"

I froze. "You know about that?"

"Well, yeah. You booked it out of there, but Norman told us about how he offered you a job."

I pursed my lips. "What exactly did he tell you?" I highly doubted Logan would act this chill if he knew the whole story, but then again, he was quite possibly hammered.

"He said you were going to be starting Monday, that you were going to help prep the space, do some outreach and publicity."

"Yeah, about that."

A bang sounded on the door through the phone. "Lo-gan," a girl sang out. "Are you hiding?"

Match to fuse, take two. "We can talk about this later," I snapped.

"What? Wait—"

"This is a bad time. You're mid—whatever. I'll figure it out."

"Crystal, hang on—"

"It's fine," I lied. "Talk later."

"Crys—"

I hung up.

I thunked the phone into the cradle and scrubbed my face with my hands. Tash gave me a disapproving look, but before she could start in on her sure-to-be rousing speech, the phone rang.

She snatched it up. "Hello?" Her eyes grew wide, and I tried to listen in, but she darted out of my reach, stretching the phone cord around the kitchen wall. "Wait, how did you get this number?" She grinned, mouthing "He called *69!" Then said, "This is Tash. Crystal called from my place."

"Tash!" I hissed.

She curled further into herself, blocking me by crushing the phone between her face and the wall. "Right, so you'll go like you're coming onto campus, stay on the main drive and take a right on Bailey." Tash nodded, giving me a stiff arm. "Yep, follow that up, then through the little roundabout—"

"Tash!" It was more of a command this time, because she was giving out directions to my house.

"It's the blue fourplex—"

I successfully snagged the cord and pulled, yanking the receiver from her grasp. We scrabbled for it on the floor, and by the time I got it close to my ear, I heard, "Think I lost you. Alright, thanks!"

The line went dead.

I reeled on her, the lower half of our bodies still tangled together. "You gave Logan directions?"

She couldn't even pretend to keep the look of sheer, diabolical gratification off her face. "You'd better get home. He's coming over."

CHAPTER
Seven

LOGAN KNOCKED TWICE before I could rush to the door. Jenna and Lindsey were both in the kitchen, and I didn't know how I was going to get out of this situation unscathed. They would recognize him immediately, considering his face had been all over the school paper since the semester started.

I cracked the door, and the cold slid past my ankles.

"Who's that?" Jenna called out.

"No one!" I snapped back.

He stood there, hair damp with snow melt, holding two Tim's coffees like a peace offering. The storm had indeed rolled in, a little later than expected.

"What are you doing here?" I hissed. "Weren't you hosting a party?"

Logan shrugged. "It was at my house, but I wasn't really the host."

"So they're all still there?"

"Probably."

"And you just . . . left?"

He nodded. Shifting on his feet. The night pressed in blue and grainy behind him, streetlight trapped in the drifting flakes.

Who walked out of a party at their own house because some

random girl from their old college phoned them? Logan Kemp made absolutely zero sense to me.

"Can you pull your hood up or something?" I hissed.

He peered over my shoulder, and I moved to block his view of Jenna and Lindsey. "You're embarrassed to be seen with me?"

"Something like that," I muttered. "Just hide your face, okay?" If they saw Logan here, I was never going to hear the end of it. It wasn't like they were friends with Sharla, but still. The fewer people who knew about this weird rendezvous, the better. Because it was only going to get weirder.

Logan pulled up the hood on his coat, and I stepped back to let him in. He took off his shoes, already coated with a layer of snow, and I barely managed to hustle him through the living room before Jenna and Lindsey realized what I was doing.

"Wait, is he sleeping over?" Jenna asked right as Lindsey said, "You didn't close the front door!"

Oops. I shoved Logan into my bedroom and ran back to remedy the situation.

"You're not going to introduce us?" Jenna stood with a hand planted on her hip.

"No introduction necessary." I scrambled for an explanation. "It's a business thing."

Lindsey's eyes widened. "Like, what kind of business?"

I locked the door and strode back through the room to the hall. "No, nothing sketchy, I promise. It's an art thing."

Jenna still looked skeptical. "Did he convince you to strip for a self-portrait or something?"

"Nope, but I wish I could make money sitting bare-assed on a stool." I waved at the two of them, then slipped into my room to, "*If he tells you to touch his penis for a promotion, say no!*"

Definitely Jenna on that one. She'd worked at a spa run by an old European dude for about three weeks over the summer until he made it clear just what he expected from his staff.

"She's right. Always say no to that." Logan stood barely a foot in front of me. I shut the door, and the space shrank by half.

My bedroom wasn't big on a good day. Single bed with a quilt my mom made me, thrift-store dresser, and a desk. With Logan there, the walls leaned in to eavesdrop.

Melted snow still clung to the ends of his hair as he shrugged off his coat, then picked up the Tim's cups he'd set on my dresser. "It's decaf."

I took one. The cup was hot against my fingers. "Thanks." My heart was already beating like I'd taken a shot of espresso. *Why was Logan here?* And why couldn't I stop thinking about whatever girl was chasing him down at his party? Again, so many questions.

Logan sat on the edge of my bed, and it protested with a squeak. I tried to perch myself on the lip of the desk, which resulted in my knocking a jar of pens onto the floor. There wasn't room for me to pull out the chair with Logan's knees in the way, so after picking up after myself, I shuffled over and leaned against the dresser.

"I'm not going to bite." Logan patted the bed next to him.

I hesitated, then flipped off the lid to my cup to buy myself some time. I breathed in the scent of dark roast to clear my nose of his cologne, then blew on the top. "There's something I have to tell you—"

"I got that much."

"But you didn't have to come over here."

He took a sip of his coffee, shifting on the bed. "The party wasn't really my jam."

I raised an eyebrow. "Oh? Hot girls throwing themselves all over you isn't really your thing?" I forced myself not to tag on "anymore" at the end of the sentence.

"You don't know if they were hot."

I snorted and took a sip of coffee, burning the tip of my tongue.

"Why did you phone me?"

Guilt burrowed behind my ribs and made a nest. "I have something to tell you."

"Yup, still with you there."

I set the coffee down so I wouldn't be tempted to scald the remainder of my virgin mouth. "I—Norman had a few misconceptions. About the whole meeting yesterday."

His eyebrows lifted, just a fraction.

I continued, "He thought—I'm not sure what gave him this impression, but he thought that you and I were . . . together."

Logan cocked his head to the side. "Huh."

My eyes narrowed. "What do you mean, 'huh?'" The way he said it made my hackles rise.

"I don't know."

"Is it so out of the realm of possibility that someone like me would be dating an NHL player?"

Logan held up a hand. "I didn't mean it like that."

"What did you mean by it?"

"I don't know, you said you weren't sure what gave him that impression, so I was agreeing with you."

I pursed my lips. This wasn't going well. I was too on edge, and Logan was . . . Logan. Confusing and annoying and hot. Not a great combination for me, it turned out. "Norman thought we were together, so he offered me the job because it includes some press opportunities and outreach. Both of which he assumed we'd be doing together. He only gave me the opportunity because he thought you came with it."

There. I said it. I picked up my coffee cup and stared into the muddy liquid. He'd added cream and sugar. Exactly how I liked it.

When Logan didn't say anything, I risked a glance up. He was grinning at me. "You signed it."

"I—" I snapped my mouth closed. He looked exactly opposite of what I expected. I had responses ready for anger and betrayal, but glee? I was at a loss. "I did. I signed it."

"You've been giving me shit about being selfish and not being honest with Shar—"

"I get it!" I groaned, clutching my cup like a comfort blanket. "But this is a little different, okay? He put me on the spot!"

"And that girl in Ontario didn't put me on the spot?"

"Dude, you kissed *more than one other girl* while you were dating Shar! This is so not the same!"

"I think the Bible would disagree. And making up a story about me in my absence—"

"For the love! Are you seriously getting all religious on me?" I turned my back on him, my cheeks on fire. I set my cup on the dresser and started organizing the clothes I still hadn't folded from laundry day. "I'm sorry, okay? I was blinded by my own ambition, and I wasn't thinking straight because it was Norman frigging Marcus!" I threw a sweater onto the bed in frustration. "I'll phone him. I'll tell him he misunderstood, and if he takes away the job—"

"No." Logan was laughing—*laughing*—as he stood and pressed his large hands onto my shoulders. I froze, tilting my head to look at him. "This is perfect. And I'm going to tell you why."

LOGAN WAITED for me to grab the contract and sit on the bed, then handed me my coffee and dropped down beside me. The mattress dipped, making me sway into him. I tried to scooch over, but our knees were still touching.

"I've got this clause," he said. "Community involvement. Team wants more outreach. Hospital visits, youth camps, whatever. It's supposed to make us look good after last season's mess."

It took me a minute, but then I remembered Axel and Rory talking about the Blizzard at Ranchman's at the end of last season. Officially, it was "an off-ice incident during the final road trip." Unofficially, half the roster got blind drunk at a sponsor's retreat in Kelowna and managed to burn every bridge between here and the Okanagan. A few players crashed a corporate yacht party, and there were reports of one player saying unrepeatable things to a Canada Parks employee when she told him to put his pants back on. The RCMP got involved when someone called about naked men singing Alanis Morissette's 'Ironic.'"

He gave me a look. "Yeah. That one. Anyway, if I do Marcus Foundation stuff or attend events, it's logged as community service hours. The PR team is happy, and you get to have your job opportunity."

Logan shifted, and his knee rubbed against mine. My skin started to buzz, but I ignored it and spun my coffee cup in my hands. "Okay, but have you looked at the dates?" There were only four. Not the end of the world, but Logan could very well be booked for any or all of them.

November 10th, Donor breakfast
November 15th, Mixer, Palliser Hotel
November 21st, TBD
December 12th, Gallery press reception
January 6th, Grand opening

"I'd have to look at my calendar at home, but I think he did his homework. Those weeks are home games."

That made sense. If Norman's plan was to use Blizzard players to secure more donors and sponsors, he definitely would've worked around their game schedule.

I worried my lower lip. "What about your parents?" I wouldn't have to tell anyone if I didn't want to. Norman only wanted Logan there, so I was hoping I could fade into the background at these events and nobody would be the wiser. But him? His mom was already involved with this project. Norman was bound to say something at some point if we didn't correct him.

He huffed a laugh. "Are you kidding? She'll be thrilled. If I got involved with a good cause? Yeah." Logan leaned back on the bed. "After Juniors, she was more pissed about the press than Shar was."

"Really?"

He nodded. "She's—look, my parents are religious. Old-school. Church every Sunday, bake sales, 'honour thy mother and father' and all that. She hated the pictures. Said I'd humiliated her."

I frowned. That's what she cared about? I chose my next words carefully. "Did Shar ever meet them?"

Logan nodded. "A couple of times."

"Huh."

Logan gave me a look.

"What?"

"You're allowed to say it but I'm not?"

I rolled my eyes. "I just meant, it's weird that they weren't worried about her, you know?"

Logan wet his lips. "Yeah. They didn't exactly approve."

"Of Shar?" My eyes flew wide.

"Of anyone who's not a good Christian girl with a chastity belt and a promise ring."

I turned on the bed, tucking my leg under me. "I mean, Shar's pretty close."

"We were living together."

Oh yeah. Good point. "Well. They'll love me, then. I'm not living in sin. I haven't lived in sin ever."

Logan's face split into a smile. "You've never lived with a guy?"

"Nope." I answered a little too proudly, then tried to backpedal. "Not because I didn't have options, it just didn't ever—"

"You don't have to explain yourself." He was still watching me, amused. I suddenly felt like a teenager trying to look cool in front of my older brother's friends. "Do you . . . you know. Date?"

I scoffed. "Of course I date." True and also misleading. I didn't remember the last time I went on an honest-to-goodness date with a guy. "I had a lovely night staying over at the hotel with Jake from Vancouver last year at the invitational."

Logan's eyes widened, and heat crawled up my neck.

"You know. For example." I wanted to bury my head under my pillow. Why had I announced that?

"Jake. Wait, was he one of their forwards?"

I nodded.

"And you hooked up with him?"

I held my hands over my face. "Can we stop talking about this, please?"

"No, I'm just wondering why him. He didn't seem all that impressive."

"He was hot, okay? And it's not like I was getting anywhere with guys on our team."

Logan turned further to mirror my position and leaned in. "Did you want to?"

"No!" I pushed off the bed.

"But if you did, who would it be?"

"Stop! Seriously. I'm not—I've never been into any of the guys on the team. It was the invitational, and it was probably a full moon. It was a moment of weakness."

"It's not weakness to want to connect with someone."

I set my almost-empty coffee down and pressed my hands to my hips. "Thank you, Dr. Kemp. Are we done now?"

He smirked. "I don't know, are we? I think, as your current boyfriend—"

I jumped forward and pressed my hands against his mouth. "Can you not talk so loud?"

Logan grabbed my wrists and threw me to the bed. I gasped, landing with a bounce and accidentally pulling him with me. He fell forward with a grunt, his body curled over mine, that grin across his face.

It was no wonder that Shar fell for him. The way his eyes lit up when he smiled with those long lashes . . .

"I knew you were embarrassed by me."

I tried to catch my breath, extremely aware of his hip pressed into mine. I was going to have to be very, very careful. Four events. Well, five, including the gallery opening, which I would've planned to attend anyway.

"There's one other thing," Logan said.

"I swear, if you say I have to touch your penis—"

He let out a guttural laugh. "That's who I am, right?"

I slipped my hands from his and scooted back, moving out from under him. When I was free and clear, I sat cross-legged. Logan didn't move. He leaned on his forearms, his legs hanging off the edge of the bed.

"I think you have to stop that," I murmured. Logan didn't answer, so I went on. "You made some really shitty mistakes when you were with Sharla. You apologized to her, right?"

He wet his lips and nodded.

"Cool. And I signed away four nights of your life and called your relationship judgment into question, so maybe we can just . . . I don't know. Start over."

Logan watched me. "You said it yourself. You and me. Not the same."

"We're not." I fiddled with one of the ties on my quilt. "But we're not, not the same." I hated to admit it, and I wasn't making excuses for him, but I understood a little of what he might've experienced at Juniors. When you had goals and ambitions and you had to make other people happy to get there—

"You know that girl in the photo?" Logan cleared his throat, dropping his eyes.

"The one in the school paper?"

He nodded, his hair falling over his forehead. "She was my coach's daughter." He let out a puff of air. "You'd think that meant I should've stayed away from her, but he treated her like a princess. She got whatever she wanted, and what she wanted . . . "

"Was you," I finished.

Logan sniffed. "Yeah." He drew a deep breath and rolled onto his back, resting his head on his arm. His fingers were inches from mine, and the urge to reach out and hold them was strong enough, I had to shove my hands in my armpits.

"The other girl, she kissed me. I was drunk. I knew I was being flirty, but I wasn't planning to do anything. It just felt good to be liked, I guess. And I was lonely, away from Shar and all. And then she was on me, and I didn't stop it right away."

I wondered how many people he'd talked to about this. Considering he hadn't spoken much to Rob and the guys, I was guessing not many. "What did Rob say to you?"

Logan sighed. "Rob kicked my ass. At practice. He told me to stop making excuses and own the hell up." He lifted his free hand and ran it through his hair. "I miss them, you know? Rob, Shar, even Rory's dumbass jokes. I torched all of that."

Pressure built behind my eyes. "Yeah. I know. I miss them, too."

Logan tilted his head to look back, but he couldn't quite meet my eyes.

I shifted forward and swivelled so we could see each other. "You weren't totally wrong about me losing my friends. They're still my friends, but it isn't the same."

He considered this. "Is she happy?"

We both knew who he was talking about. "She's stupidly happy. It's pretty gross, actually." Logan chuckled, and I couldn't tell if the look on his face was relief or hurt. "Are *you* happy?"

He looked away, staring at the ceiling. "I'm an NHL player. I'm all successful and shit." He shot me a look, and I laughed. *He remembered that from the grocery store?* "Of course I'm happy."

"Well, good. Then I guess—"

The door to my room busted open. "Hey, do you know where —?" Jenna froze. She stared at Logan stretched out on the bed. "Um, Crystal? Why is Logan Kemp in your bedroom?"

CHAPTER
Nine

AFTER ATTENDING my morning classes on Monday, I drove straight over to the warehouse. In Jenna's car this time. Rob and Sharla were back from the tournament. Maddie filled me in when we met up outside the cafeteria. Douglas took third, which was right in line with what they'd hoped, considering all the new blood on the team. Of course, it had to be Maddie's numbers that accomplished that.

My "orientation" had been about three minutes of discussion with Norman's assistant and one gesture at a mountain of boxes. I found the supply closet and committed to being the world's best art janitor.

By two-oh-five, I'd already inhaled enough dust to qualify for a miner's pension. Norman's warehouse smelled like wet concrete and old coffee, with a top note of varnish that made the back of my tongue feel weirdly minty. They'd have to mitigate that before the opening.

Thankfully, my Walkman made all my tasks manageable. After breaking down boxes for over an hour, I was in the process of flipping my mix tape when I heard footsteps.

I spun to see Logan approaching. "What are you doing here?" I pulled my headphones off.

His mom, Alice, walked up behind him. Hair neat, pea coat perfectly pressed. She carried a bag full of what looked to be blue painter's tape and a label maker.

"Morning," she said warmly. "First day. Congratulations."

"Thanks." I shoved the tape back into its slot and clicked the Walkman tray closed.

She looked between the two of us and said, "Alright. Well, you two have fun," then spun on her heel and walked back toward Norman's makeshift office.

Logan bounced on his heels, all six feet and change of testosterone-fueled muscle. "Where do you want me?"

It took me a second to process the sentence. "Uh, right now?"

"Thought I'd pitch in. Norman's got board people touring."

"Your mom told you that?"

He smirked. "Technically, you did. Because why wouldn't I want to spend time with my girlfriend after practice?"

My lips drew into a line. "Is this what we're doing?" After talking Jenna and Lindsey down last night, swearing them to secrecy, and barely getting to sleep around two, I was not mentally prepared to adjust my game plan.

I'd geared myself up for four events with Logan. Four times we had to pretend to be together, that was it. But if he was going to show up every day that I went to work? If Norman was there? *Was he going to have to touch me?*

"Norman Marcus doesn't know your practice schedule," I hissed, handing him a broom. I picked up the box cutter and went back to work.

"Oh. So you don't want me here?"

I levelled my gaze at him, knife at the ready. "If your mom's here, I'm assuming he is, too?" Logan nodded. "Right, so he's going to . . . you know. Expect us to look like a couple."

It was impossible to whisper in here. The smallest sound echoed. Thankfully, Logan's sweeping made a good white noise buffer. "We're just working."

"And when we're not?"

He bent over to pick up a piece of packing tape stuck to the floor. "We just need to come up with ground rules."

"Perfect." I sliced through the next box, folded it flat and tossed it on the pile. "How about no photos."

"Like, ever? Aren't we going to press—"

"Yes, but the only reason I'm here is to get you to come, which I still don't understand, by the way."

Logan frowned, resting his hands on the broom handle. "Why do you think that?"

"That's what Norman Marcus said."

"Can you stop with the name?"

"It's his name, Logan. It's like Celine Dion. You have to say both."

He resumed sweeping. "I would've come to those events. My mom is being featured here."

"That's what I assumed, but then he made it sound like I would have to convince you. He said I had you wrapped around my finger."

Logan winced, then muttered a few choice curse words under his breath.

I paused mid box cut. "What?"

He set the broom handle against the wall and went back for the dust pan. "I think this is Alice's doing."

"Your mom?"

"Yeah. My mom." He flipped his hat around backward and dropped into a squat, trying to hold the dust pan with one hand and maneuver the broom with the other.

"Stop." I dropped the box cutter and jogged over. He handed me the broom, and we worked together to clean up the pile.

Logan dumped it into the trash bag. "My parents were at the game the other night. They saw . . . a few unfortunate things in the stands. Douglas girls with signs. And then they came down to the tunnel after, and you know, friends and girlfriends hang out there, and they always bring people along who want to go out after.

"More girls."

He had the decency to look a little chagrined. "Yep."

I started to put two and two together. If Logan's parents were upset about his pictures from World Juniors, how would they take getting a glimpse of the potential he had for hookups on a daily basis?

"But you're, what, twenty?"

He blew out a breath. "Doesn't matter. My parents won't ever stop worrying about me. With these guns—" He flexed his arm and pretended to kiss his bicep.

"Oh my gosh, stop." I shoved his shoulder and walked back to my box cave. "So what, you think your mom decided to pretend you had a girlfriend? So everyone would find out and you'd be pressured to stay celibate?" I snorted. "Didn't they see what happened last time?"

I tried to swallow the words as they were coming out, but couldn't stop them. My head shot up. "I'm sorry, Logan, I didn't mean—"

"It's good."

"It's not good. You told me what happened, and then I put you right back in that box." I lifted the half-disassembled cardboard next to me for emphasis.

Logan's mouth twitched like he was hiding a smile. "Well. I guess you're just a terrible person."

"This has already been established."

Logan looked like he was going to say something, but didn't. He picked up the broom and moved to my side of the room. "So. Rules."

Right. I was more than glad for the change of subject until I remembered what had distracted us. If Logan's mom had put this whole thing into place so Logan would be held accountable, could I still avoid taking photos without causing a problem?

My heart started to race. Every time Logan was in the press, it was blasted across Douglas U. I couldn't be in a picture with him without the entire campus finding out. "I don't want to do photos."

He nodded. "Okay. What are we going to say?"

"That I believe cameras steal souls?"

Logan blinked. "You're going to pretend to be Indigenous?"

"Or Amish." Either way, it sounded bad when I said it out loud. "Okay, maybe not. How about that I'm super insecure and have body image issues."

Logan made a sound in his throat. "You have pink hair, Crystal. Not the choice you'd make if you wanted to blend into the background."

"Maybe I'm overcompensating. And besides, artists are always odd ducks. I could be expressing myself only for me, you know? This isn't for other people." I gestured at my highlights.

Logan laughed. "Where do you even come up with that?"

I tapped my head. "It gets weird in here. You're lucky I have a filter."

"Not good enough to keep the Logan insults at bay."

I flinched. "I said I was sorry!"

"Kidding, it's fine."

He pushed the broom, and dirt clouded between us. I coughed and stepped back, waiting for it to settle.

"Okay, no photos. What else?"

"No touching. Unless we absolutely have to." I moved to the other side of the mountain and started there.

"Why would we have to?" Logan waggled an eyebrow.

"You're impossible." His grin only widened, and a thought hit me square in the chest. Was this how he was with Shar? I thought back to every moment at Ranchman's. Logan was larger than life, but was his attention ever on her like this? Maybe it was like this in the beginning. His charm was turned up to the max, and then once they were together—once he'd gotten what he wanted—he didn't have to try so hard.

"You okay?" Logan paused his sweeping.

I waved him off. "Oh, yeah. Just a brain fart."

He didn't seem convinced, but I ignored him and started in on a box that must've held a refrigerator. "We might have to touch if we're walking somewhere together or we're sitting beside each other for a long time. To make it look realistic."

"Got it. So you're talking an arm around the shoulder or holding hands?"

I cringed. "Who holds hands?"

"Wow. Jake from Vancouver must've been a real romantic."

I picked up a box the size of my head and threw it at him. It died and landed at his feet. "That's what you get."

Logan chortled and picked up the box, chucking it back at me. His throw would've done some damage if I hadn't dodged.

"What about kissing?" He asked, lobbing another box my direction.

"Hard pass."

"Second base?"

"You play hockey. No need for bases." I ducked behind a pillar and kicked a box at his head. Logan caught it, but barely.

"Perfect. So straight to the net, eh?"

"Ugh. You would." I pressed myself flat behind the pillar, but when nothing flew past after a few seconds, I braved a look. That ended with me screaming and stumbling back because Logan was inches in front of my face with a box in his hands.

"Shit! Crystal, what—" Logan dropped the box and lunged after me, grabbing my arm before I fell completely on my ass.

When I found my footing, I smacked him in the chest. "You scared the crap out of me!"

"Ow! You started it!" Logan tugged on my arm, pulling me close and giving me a nougie.

"Logan!" I pressed my fingers into his sides to get free, but that only made him squeeze tighter, locking my arms to my sides while I laughed until I could barely breathe. "Logan, I'm going to pass out!"

"Don't tickle me," he laughed, breathless.

"I wasn't! I swear!"

He loosened his grip, but as soon as I moved, he locked down again.

"I'm not going to do it!" I sucked in a breath and pushed back, finally getting some separation, when a voice from across the room made me jump.

"Creating a mosaic?"

I jumped to attention, recognizing Norman's tone before I spotted him. He stood back by the broom, two men with him. Both with camera equipment.

"We hoped we could get a photo for documentation? The floor goes in at the end of the week, and then we're on to trim, finishing touches, and my favourite part. The artwork." He beamed at us.

Heat climbed my neck. How much had he seen? "Um, sure. Let me just get out of the way—"

Norman clicked his tongue. "I want both of you in it, please."

I looked to Logan with a panicked expression, but what was he supposed to do?

"Come a little closer," Norman said, pointing to a spot in front of the now deconstructed pile of boxes. We obeyed, and he gave a satisfied nod.

Then, as the men lifted their cameras, Logan leaned down, picked up a box, and dropped it directly over my head.

Norman said something, but Logan only chuckled. "It's artistic. People will love it."

I couldn't have wiped the grin off my face if I tried.

The rest of the week unspooled in typical fashion with notable highlights. I completed my armature in the pottery studio and was mostly happy with it. These days, that was the highest compliment. I attended an excellent Art History lecture, slept better than usual, and Norman reached out to see if I could help with some administrative tasks like organizing and responding to some of his emails.

I'd be lying if I said I didn't find all of it fascinating. Once he gave me access, I read every single message, sometimes scrolling back in the chain for months. Logan was on a week-long away game tour. Ottawa, Toronto, and one game south of the border.

By Friday afternoon, I was home alone, wearing socks and drinking tea. It couldn't have been more idyllic before the pounding on the front door started. I debated ignoring it completely, but this person didn't walk away after a minute. Or three.

I finally got up and opened it to find Maddie, hair in a ponytail, eyes flashing. She held up the *Calgary Herald* like a cop flashing a badge, and my stomach clenched.

Front page of the City section, there was a photo of me and Logan at the warehouse, but not the one with the box on my head. I was in his arms, both of our faces thrown back and shaped by laughter.

The caption was in bold: BLIZZARD STAR LOGAN KEMP AND DOUGLAS UNIVERSITY STUDENT PITCH IN AS NEW GALLERY TAKES SHAPE. The subhead: 'Young artist' and Kemp's girlfriend, Crystal MacMillan, leads the charge.

Maddie tapped her foot on the steps. "Explain."

CHAPTER

Ten

THE *CALGARY HERALD* lay spread on the coffee table between us, my stupid face squinched and laughing, and Logan's grin making it look like we're hopelessly devoted.

"Start talking." Maddie tapped the paper.

I pressed my hands into my thighs until my fingers went white. "Do you remember how Logan mentioned Norman Marcus at the grocery store? When we were checking out?"

Maddie looked skeptical. She didn't know the name, so it probably hadn't stuck.

"He's high up in the art world here, like everyone knows him, and Logan's family has a connection. Did you know his mom is an artist? Professional artist. She has her work in galleries all over Alberta."

"I don't see how this has to do with you making out—"

"We weren't making out! I promise! Logan followed up after we went shopping, and he offered to introduce me to Mr. Marcus." This is where the story became more difficult to tell. But Maddie had the most damning piece of evidence in front of her, so there was no point holding back. "He offered me a job, which is huge because it could lead to an entry-level gallery position. That's all I've ever wanted—"

"I thought you were going to go get your master's?" Her face softened the tiniest bit.

"I said that because I didn't think it was possible for me to get an in at a gallery, but I don't want to do more school."

Maddie nodded. "Yeah. I was surprised you were planning to do another two years."

It wasn't a dig, just the truth. I endlessly complained about homework, especially group projects, which was exactly what a master's would look like. Maddie should know. "Exactly. But I didn't realize that the only reason Mr. Marcus was offering me the position was because . . . he thought Logan and I were together."

"Why would he think that?"

I sank into the couch, blowing out a breath. "We have no idea."

"We?"

"Logan and I. I signed the contract because it seemed like if I walked out of that room, the opportunity would never come again, but it locked us in to attending these press events, and it turns out that Logan's super lonely—"

"Okay, but that's his fault!"

"No, I know, but then I found out his mom may have been the one to insinuate that we were dating when she set up the appointment for me because she thinks Logan's a man-whore—"

"Which he is."

I bristled at that comment. "I don't know, Maddie. I think . . ." I shook my head, not sure how to say it.

"You think what?" Maddie's face frowned in disgust.

We were supposed to hate Logan Kemp, and I didn't want to break the girlfriend code, but Logan's explanations made sense. I folded my arms, giving myself a preemptive hug in preparation for what I had to say next. "I think people do things because they think it's the only way to get what they want, even if it isn't always right."

"So you're justifying what he did?"

I squeezed my eyes shut. "No. I'm saying I'm almost as bad."

"Crystal—"

"I signed the contract, agreeing to the press appearances without telling him, Maddie. I pretended Norman was right, that Logan and I were together because I didn't want to lose the job."

"That's not the same thing."

"No, but it's close! Logan was under pressure with his coach and his team, he thought he had to be Mr. Cool to get good recommendations to agents and teams. So yeah, what he did was crappy, but I don't know. I understand a little of why he did it."

Maddie considered for a moment. "So you told Logan?"

I nodded. "He said it was a perfect setup. I guess he has some PR clause in his contract because of all the shenanigans in the spring."

"Oh, yeah, those Blizzard players?"

I nodded again. "We think his mom is trying to keep his image pure or something. Make it seem like he's got a home-town girlfriend, and Norman is doing some exhibit with hockey. I don't understand why it's so important to have Blizzard players at the events, but he's making it a huge priority. I told Logan I wasn't going to do photos. I didn't want to make this a big thing. I thought I could just do my time and pretend I was with him until the press walk through, then we could break up and I could move on with a position at the gallery, but I don't think Norman Marcus cares about me. He wants Logan and he thought I was the way to get him—"

"Uh, I think he cares." Maddie pulled the paper toward her, searched for something in the text, and when she found it, held it out for me to read.

The upcoming Marcus Arts Foundation Gallery took another step toward reality this week as founder Norman Marcus announced an ambitious bid for a provincial matching grant from Alberta's Arts and Culture Fund. To strengthen the application, Marcus has begun a formal partnership with Douglas University, citing the need for "emergent voices" and "meaningful student involvement" in the province's cultural future.

"The government wants proof that the next generation is engaged," Marcus said during a brief walk-through of the converted warehouse space. "That's why artists like Douglas student Crystal MacMillan are essential. She represents exactly what Alberta's art community can become—fresh, earnest, and rooted in the city's future."

After last year's funding cuts, the province has emphasized "student-centred initiatives" in awarding grants—something Marcus appears more than ready to capitalize on…

The newspaper crinkled in my hand. What the hell? Norman was using me as proof that he was "student-centric" to get a provincial grant? *I was essential?*

I dropped the paper to the table. "Do you know what I did on my first day?" I turned to Maddie, my chest on fire. "I broke down boxes. I've had absolutely zero to do with anything related to art or 'the province's cultural future.'"

Maddie took the paper from me before I crumpled it up and tossed it on the floor. "So. Norman Marcus is an asshat."

It seemed that way. I guess this is what they meant by "don't meet your heroes?" But the fact remained that he was also a very powerful and well-connected asshat.

"And what about the picture?" Maddie asked.

I groaned and pinched the bridge of my nose. "We were having a box fight."

"What?"

"A box fight. Like throwing boxes at each other. It sounds idiotic, but he scared the hell out of me and I fell, and . . . I have no idea how they got this photo, but I wasn't making out with him. I wasn't anything with him. We're just—" I slumped over my knees. "I don't know what we are. Allies?"

Maddie's expression was more thoughtful than disgruntled, but there was still judgment there. I deserved it.

"I don't know why you didn't say something." Maddie swept a loose curl from her cheek.

"Really?" I gave her a look, and she cracked a smile.

"Okay, I get why you didn't tell Shar, but why didn't you tell me?"

That was a fair question. "I don't know." And that was a lie. But how could I tell her that since she'd gotten together with Chase, our relationship hadn't felt the same? Without sounding like a petty, jealous friend? Which I definitely was at least some of the time.

Thankfully, I didn't have to elaborate. Saved by the phone ringing.

I jumped up from the couch. "Sorry, I'll be right back." I slid into the kitchen and grabbed the phone. "Hello?"

"Hey, Crystal?" Rob's voice. He sounded frantic.

My heart jumped into my throat. "What's wrong?"

"Who is it?" Maddie appeared next to me.

I gripped the phone tighter. "Rob—?"

"Shar's in labour. We're at the hospital. They have her in a room, I don't know. She's in a lot of pain, but they won't let me go back—"

"Which hospital?" I scrambled for my notepad. Maddie handed me the pen I knocked across the countertop.

Rob stuttered through the name, and I'd barely hung up when Maddie grabbed my arm. "C'mon. I'm driving."

SOFT BEEPS from the heart monitor blended with the buzz of the fluorescent lighting. The smell of antiseptic clung to everything, including our hands, since Maddie and I had to wash before taking up residence on the ugly beige couch across from Shar's bed.

None of it mattered. Because Shar was cradling the most perfect human I'd ever seen against her chest, her hair plastered to her forehead in wet curls, cheeks flushed, eyes half-mooned with exhaustion and triumph. Shar was glowing. Not metaphorically, but literally. Sweat and joy and an otherworldly shimmer.

The baby stretched, tiny fingers unfurling and clenching. The three of us held our breath, enraptured.

Carter Robert Thompson. Born at 7:05 pm, nineteen inches long, and weighing seven pounds, eleven ounces. Those numbers meant nothing to me, but I had already memorized them.

"I can't get over how small he is," Maddie whispered, leaning close. We'd both had a chance to hold him after Shar lied to the nurse and told her we were her blood sisters to get us into the room. She looked skeptical, but Maddie held her ground, daring her to make things awkward with a racial comment.

Maddie told us after that she had an adoption sob story all lined up, just in case.

Rob's voice filtered in from the nurse's station right outside the door. "Yes, his name is Carter Robert. No, you'll have to wait —yeah, wait til tomorrow . . . "

Shar sighed, beaming. "He hasn't stopped since Carter arrived. I swear, he's called every single person we've ever met."

Carter stretched then, his face scrunching like he was in the middle of a bad dream. Maddie made a noise like a wounded goose, and Shar smoothed the little creases between his brows with her fingertip.

"Shar? Babe?" Rob stuck his head in. His eyes were bloodshot, his shirt inside out. "Your mom wants to know if three o'clock is okay tomorrow.

Shar grinned. "Yes." As soon as Rob left, her smile slipped. "I feel so bad."

"About what?" Maddie asked.

"He's calling my entire family, and he has nobody." Her eyes grew glassy. "Here we have this perfect miracle, and he can't even share it with anyone."

That sobered me. Rob lost his mom when he was young, and his dad was a deadbeat if I remembered correctly. "What about his siblings?"

Shar shrugged. "I'm sure he'll try them. Maybe his sister. Their family just isn't close." She chewed on her lower lip, then lowered her eyes to Carter. "We're going to change that. We're going to have the closest, best family. Rob deserves that."

"You're going to have more kids?" I asked.

Shar's face lit up. "Are you kidding? I'd do this again in a second."

Maddie laughed out loud. "Are you remembering the last three hours? Rob said he's never heard you scream like that."

Shar scoffed. "I mean, a watermelon was coming out of my hoo-haw. Hell yes, I screamed." She kissed the top of Carter's head. "Totally worth it."

My eyes misted up.

Shar lay back against the pillows, eyes fluttering between us and the baby like she couldn't get enough of any of it. For a moment, the three of us just breathed, revelling in the soft hush around us.

It didn't last nearly long enough.

"So are we going to talk about the picture?" Shar looked up with a glint in her eye.

Damn it. "You saw that?"

Maddie's eyes widened. "I only saw it because Chase has a Herald subscription."

"Well, so does our next-door neighbour, Mrs. Makar, and she's also out of town. Rob went to bring her paper in so it wouldn't get wet when the snow melted."

"Do you think everyone saw it?"

"No," Shar said, right as Maddie said, "Maybe?"

I didn't know if it was the hospital room or the sheer perfection of Shar and Carter sitting in that bad, but the emotional dam I'd built talking to Maddie burst in an instant. Tears filled my eyes. "I'm an idiot."

Maddie scooted closer, pulling me against her.

I told them everything, and I mean everything. Starting with making out with Garrett over the summer, because that shameful secret had been living in my body unchecked for too long, and then the rest came tumbling out.

How alone I'd felt after they both got together with Rob and Chase, how I'd tried to make new friends, to hang out with Tash and her group, but it didn't feel the same, and I missed them, but it wasn't their fault because of course it wasn't, and then the whole deal with Logan. How he called and wanted to help, and I was a complete self-righteous D-bag to him, and then I pulled the most selfish move without owning up to it.

How I'd wanted to keep it a secret because it was Logan and it wasn't even real and I never in a million years wanted to hurt Shar, but I didn't know what I was going to do after graduation and I felt like a complete and utter failure, and now I was selling my soul to get in with Norman Marcus who I was quickly finding out was also using me to link up with Douglas for grant money.

"The whole thing is a pile of steaming dog poo, and I'm the worst friend in the world!" I finished with true dramatic flair.

Shar and Maddie stared at me a moment, stunned. Then Shar let out a breath. "Wow."

"I know!" I splayed out over the back of the couch like a dying fish.

"No, I meant, wow, like this is an amazing opportunity, Crys."

I lifted my head, skeptical. "That's what you got from all that?"

Shar didn't miss a beat. "Yes! Let's be strategic, here. If Norman—super weird that he has the same name as my dad, by the way—is using you, then why shouldn't you use him back? And this is helping Logan, too, right? So why the hell not? Men do it all the time, so why can't we use a relationship to our advantage?"

I blinked. That was a very good point. "But it doesn't bother you? Me showing up like that with Logan? It wasn't real AT ALL—"

"I know!" Shar laughed. "And yeah, I won't lie and say it doesn't tweak something in me to think of you two spending time together. Not because I have a problem with it, just because . . . I don't know." She pondered for a moment. "I think I just don't want you to get hurt."

I snorted. "No worries there. We have rules."

"What?" Maddie laughed.

"Yep. No touching unless absolutely necessary, only four events until the opening, and then we'll have an amicable break up." I mimed washing my hands of him. "He'll get his PR credit and make his mom happy, I'll hopefully have a job offer—"

"Yeah, this is a win-win," Shar said.

Maddie nodded in agreement, her brows still pinched. "I'm just . . . so sorry, Crystal. I had no idea—"

"No, please. I promise, this is a me problem."

She shook her head. "No, it's not. I know it's not our fault, I get that, but I didn't think about how our relationships affected you. I want to be better."

"But Chase needs to be your priority." I pointed at Carter. "And your two guys need to be yours."

Shar's face screwed up. "Yes. But you're family, too, Crys. I agree with Maddie. We need to make this work."

Tears rolled down my cheeks, and I pulled Maddie up from the couch for a true group hug plus one brand new, tiny human.

As soon as we pulled back, Rob pushed through the door, a tired smile on his face. "Alright. What'd I miss?"

CHAPTER
Twelve

BY THE TIME the donor breakfast officially started, I'd already refilled the coffee urn twice and alphabetized the name tags three different ways. The Rozsa Centre atrium at Douglas was dressed for brunch. Round tables with white cloths, little glass vases with maroon and gold mums, trays of pastries under domed lids. The floor-to-ceiling windows showed a winter wonderland with all the tree limbs kissed with frost.

On the far side of the room, Norman worked the donors like a man competing in speed chess. Three conversations at once, all easy smiles and pointed comments. Two university administrators, one from Advancement, one from Fine Arts, hovered like vultures. A *Calgary Herald* photographer lingered near the entrance, fiddling with his flash.

The one saving grace of this event was that the Outlaws hockey team and seniors in my major were invited. Plus, Logan hadn't arrived yet. Winning all around.

I grinned as Maddie appeared in the doorway. She waltzed over with Chase in tow. "This looks amazing!"

I laughed and gave her a hug. "It better. I'm getting paid by the hour." Really, I hadn't been given much responsibility. With a few midterms last week, I didn't have spare time, and since I was now aware Norman needed me for more than my work ethic, I didn't hesitate to tell him so. "How's Shar?"

"Blissful. Not getting much sleep."

"As expected." I was planning to stop over after the event.

"Crystal." Norman materialized at my elbow. "There you are. I've been telling the Dean of Fine Arts that you're the model of the Douglas–Marcus partnership."

Terrifying sentence. "Oh. Thank you."

The Dean, a tall woman in a blazer that cost more than my tuition, smiled. "We're thrilled you're involved. This kind of student engagement in the community is exactly what we're hoping to inspire."

I nodded, keeping my thoughts to myself on that one. Douglas hadn't done a damn thing to help me connect with the art community. Well, except give Logan a scholarship.

"Don't forget to circulate with the other art students," Norman murmured. "We'll be doing some selection for the opening show. Eyes open, ears open." Then, louder for the benefit of the photographer now creeping closer: "We're excited to find more student artwork to feature in our opening exhibit . . . " He walked away, herding the press toward more important people than me.

The tables were filling up, and I quickly found my happy place. Rob, Maddie, Axel, Rory, and the rest of the team who weren't in class or asleep sat at two rounds near the back corner. The guys looked weirdly cleaned up. I hadn't noticed before, but Rob was in a button-up shirt, sleeves rolled up, freshly shaven.

Just like my moment with Logan, I suddenly saw him as grown. *He was a father.* I had to shake my head at that one.

"You okay?" I asked, pulling out the chair next to Maddie.

She nodded. Rob smiled so wide it almost split his face. "Forgot to tell you. Carter smiled this morning."

"Wow," Axel said. "Peak."

"Shut up," Rob said, but he was grinning.

I picked up the conversation where we'd left off before Norman interrupted. "How's Chase?"

"Busy. He—" Maddie stopped mid-sentence as the noise in the room changed. The doors opened and in walked . . .

Holy shit.

Logan walked in first, donning a grey suit, black shirt with the hint of a scoop neck, looking like he'd wandered off a bill-board. Behind him was Davis Rourke, the Blizzard's hotshot twenty-two-year-old winger with a charcoal Henley, pants that hugged his incredible rear end, and a face that made half the city forgive him for never backchecking. And anchoring the trio was Mark Haines, veteran defenceman, salt-and-pepper hair, jawline that could cut glass, and the kind of status that comes with a Stanley Cup ring. Twice over.

The room reacted instantly. Heads were on swivels. Conversations stalled. A girl in a Douglas hoodie grabbed her friend's arm like all three of them were walking on water.

"A little overkill, eh?" Axel muttered.

Rory licked his thumb and tried to wipe Axel's face like a mom. Axel reacted like he'd just walked into a spiderweb.

Rory chortled. "Stop, you've just got a little green on your face. I'll get it for you!"

Axel nearly fell out of his chair, and Maddie had to grab his arm to keep him upright.

Logan skimmed the room, and when his gaze landed on me, his mouth tipped into that quick, easy smile. It slipped a little when he saw who I was sitting with, but he leaned over and said something to Rourke, then followed the edge of the room and headed our way.

Good for him.

"Hey," he said when he reached our table, hands sliding into his pockets.

"Surprised you can do that," I teased, pointing at his pants.

Rob stifled a laugh.

"What?" Logan frowned.

"Just doesn't look like much else could fit in there."

Logan realized I was talking about how tight his clothes were and smirked. "Yeah. If my package was a little smaller, maybe they'd have more give."

I groaned, and Rory guffawed. "Wow, Crystal. You two working together? Setting him up for wristers?"

"No. We're not—anything together," I stammered. Rob thankfully saved me by pushing back from the table and standing.

"Kemp." He held out a hand.

Logan looked at it a moment, but as he pulled his hand out to shake, Rob laughed and yanked him into a hug. "Too good for me, now, eh? With your fancy friends?"

Logan clapped him on the back. "Always was, dickhead." They pulled back, beaming at each other. "You're a dad."

I'd sent Logan an email letting him know, but hadn't heard back. He was gone all week on an away game tour out east.

"I am. Thanks for the diapers."

Logan dropped his hands from Rob's shoulders. "More where that came from." He pretended to check out Rob's backside. "Did I guess right on the size?"

Rob pretended to jersey him and give a few head shots. So. Back to normal, it seemed.

Campus girls were now lined up at the windows, their breath fogging the glass. "I think you might need to appear for your adoring public." I nodded toward the doors. Haines and Rourke were waving Logan over.

Maddie followed my gaze. "Did you bring your stick? You might have to beat them off with it."

Logan smirked. "I always have my stick. And I don't mind a good beating off."

Rory groaned. "What the hell, ladies? Again with the assist."

I rolled my eyes as Logan strutted back to his teammates, and I couldn't help but think about him lying on his back, his arm looped behind his head, in my bedroom.

I drew a deep breath and forced my eyes away from the V of his torso.

People finally began moving through the buffet line. Plates piled with scrambled eggs, sausages, and fresh fruit Norman must've had imported. You could never find strawberries that red in Calgary this time of year. Rob loaded up like he hadn't eaten in three days. Axel took four muffins "for later," which likely meant the walk back to class.

Logan, Rourke, and Haines signed autographs out front for over half an hour, then barely made it to the juice table before people started handing them napkins, programs, and even one girl's spiral notebook to sign. Norman hovered nearby like a proud stage mom, positioning them under the best lighting, introducing them to donors whose watches cost more than my rent.

I talked with Tash and a few other art majors I knew from my classes and returned to the Outlaws table just in time to see Jake walk over and take the seat beside Axel. There he was. Number twelve. Why did he look like that was his age and not just his number?

"MacMillan," he said with a half smile.

"Hey."

Jake scanned the room. "Surprised they didn't hold this in the cafeteria. Love that place." He gave me a wink, and my cheeks heated.

Maddie choked on her coffee. Rory's eyebrows shot up to his hairline.

Did everyone know about that?

"What's so great about the cafeteria?"

I jolted. Logan somehow stood at my side with a full plate, now looking between me and Jake. "Hey," he said, his eyes dropping to my mouth.

I shifted on my feet. "Hey, back."

Jake leaned back in his chair. "Cafeteria's the place to be. Especially after hours."

I cleared my throat, heat rising to my neck. "Um, we should find you a spot. Maybe with the donors?" I turned from the table, trying to pull Logan with me, but he didn't budge.

"What's your name, bud?" Logan asked.

"Jake."

Logan's brows lifted.

Damn it.

"Hey, Jake. Where are you from?" His jaw was tense, his chin lifted. I could've sworn he was puffing out his chest.

"Logan," I hissed. This was not the time or place to get into a pissing match, and *why did he even care?* It was a nothing comment. There was no reason to dig into this.

"Just joined the team. Transferred from Vancouver. Too bad we never got to play together."

Logan nodded. "Too bad."

Jake ran a hand through his hair, somehow oblivious. "Looking forward to the invitational this year."

I plastered a smile to my face. "I'm sure it will be great. Okay, I think—"

"Why is that? Jake from Vancouver." Logan smiled like there was nowhere else in the world he'd rather be.

My eyes flared. "Really? This is what we're doing?"

"I'm just curious. Because he's trying to flirt with you."

Jake chuckled. "Just floating an opinion, pal."

I had to give Jake credit. He didn't flinch once during this aggressive confrontation.

Logan smiled, but his eyes were steely. He raised his voice just enough so the tables adjacent to us could hear. "Yeah, see, I don't think you were. And I don't love that you're making a move on my girlfriend."

That time, Rory was the one who choked, spraying muffin crumbs all over the tablecloth.

CHAPTER
Thirteen

BY THE TIME the Dean finished her speech about "innovative partnerships" and "synergy between athletics and the arts," my face hurt. People stood, clapped politely, then scraped their chairs back. Donors began migrating toward the exit in clumps, clutching their little program booklets and making comments about "very promising young talent."

Norman hovered near the doors like a spider arranging its web. He shook hands, flattered, and steered people toward the Blizzard trio.

"Don't stab anyone," Maddie murmured, collecting plates. "I know the urge is strong."

"I make no promises." She most likely assumed I was annoyed with all the production, but the only person I truly wanted to stab was Logan. What had he been thinking? We'd discussed how I wanted to keep all of this a secret. He didn't even know that I'd talked to Shar and Maddie, which meant he totally threw me under the bus. And for what? To prove he was better than a transfer student?

I dropped my stack of paper products in the trash just as Norman's assistant appeared at my elbow. "Crystal, can I borrow you for a moment? We'd love a few more photos with the team."

Of course they would. "Sure." It was fine. I could stand beside Logan and pretend I didn't want to rip his head off.

I squeezed through the crowd toward the front of the atrium, where the Herald photographer had staged a mini setup against a maroon-and-gold banner. Logan stood with Rourke and Haines.

"Crystal." Norman beckoned. "Jump in."

I stepped into place, but didn't greet or acknowledge him. Not because I was giving him the silent treatment. Right now, I didn't trust anything that came out of my mouth where he was concerned.

"Closer," the photographer said. "Maybe hand half in your pocket? Logan, turn just a bit toward her—yes."

Logan's hand slid over my lower back, and I forced myself not to arch or flinch. *Flash.* Another angle. *Flash.*

"Perfect," the photographer said. "Can we get one with the students?"

Norman snapped his fingers, summoning a handful of art kids who'd been orbiting the coffee table all morning. Tash slipped in late, and I waved her over.

When she shook her head, I mouthed. "Get over here!"

She balked, but eventually wandered our direction. As soon as she stopped next to me, I turned to Norman and caught his attention. "Norman, this is my friend, Tash. She does printmaking. A bunch of stuff, really."

He shook her hand, then passed her a card. "We're taking submissions for the opening show. Make sure you get a description of your work to me through email."

Tash's eyebrows ticked up. "Will do." She obediently got into the group for a photo.

"One with the whole group," the photographer announced. "Blizzard, student artists, Mr. Marcus, perfect."

We arranged ourselves: Logan behind me, Tash at my other side, a row of students up front. I pasted on another smile. The flash went off again, bright enough to make a black spot in my vision.

Norman clapped his hands once. "Excellent," he said. "We've done good work this morning. Crystal, excellent work. Logan, thank you. Gentlemen," he nodded at Rourke and Haines, "a pleasure."

Tash squeezed my arm. "You good?"

"Ask me in a week."

Tash laughed. "Well, at least you look hot."

I gave her a hug, and when I saw Logan approaching, I turned and made a beeline for the front doors. I couldn't talk to him right now, I was too mad. Making a public scene at the donors breakfast was the last thing I needed to do to expand my career options.

Outside, the air was crisp and bright. The Douglas quad stretched out, patchy grass rimmed with frost, the flags at half-mast for Remembrance Day week. Students shuffled between buildings, breath fogging, backpacks bouncing.

I stomped down onto the concrete.

"Crystal," Logan called. "Hey."

I didn't turn right away. I let him catch up, because at least then we'd be far enough from the Rozsa that the cameras wouldn't be watching.

When he reached my side, I pivoted to face him. "What."

He blinked. "You're mad."

"Excellent observation."

"Can I ask why?"

Seriously? There was no way he was that clueless. I took a breath that stung my lungs. "You don't get to do that."

"Do what?" he asked, a look of genuine confusion on his face.

"Declare I'm your girlfriend. In front of my friends without asking me first."

Relief washed over him. "I was trying to help."

"By commandeering my personal life?" My voice pitched up. "You don't think maybe that's something we should have, I don't know, discussed? In private?"

He exhaled, watching his breath plume and disappear. "Jake was hitting on you, and there were people there who would notice."

"Jake hits on everyone, and nobody from the press cares about me. Norman was too busy peacocking. You're the only one who saw a thing, so don't pretend it was about that."

He scoffed. "You don't know that, and it shouldn't have been me putting him in his place. Rory or Axel or Rob should've done it. That kid isn't worth your time."

I laughed, short and sharp. "You don't get to decide that either. Maybe I enjoyed his company last spring."

His frown deepened, a muscle in his jaw tightening. "Okay."

"Okay." I crossed my arms. "I specifically told you I didn't want people at Douglas to know."

His eyes narrowed. "No you didn't."

"I—yes I did! I said I didn't want photos—"

"No photos doesn't mean you don't want people to know. Maybe—"

"You knew what I meant. And there was already a picture of us in the Herald—"

"Yeah. I saw it." He scrubbed a hand over his jaw.

I drew a breath and released it. "I need to go home. I have a project to finish."

He nodded.

"Talk to you later." I turned and walked away before he could say something to make me feel like forgiving him. It seemed like he was close, and I didn't want to hear it because now I had a decision to make. Was I going to let the entire Outlaws team think this was real? That I'd gone behind Shar's back to date her ex? Or was I going to tell them the truth?

There were already too many people who knew what Logan and I were doing, and we weren't even close to the press walk through at the gallery. Would Norman start to hear the rumors? Especially if he was working with other students at Douglas? Would he care?

Variables swam in my subconscious as I trudged toward home. Logan Kemp had simultaneously improved my life and complicated it. I didn't have enough information yet to decide if any of it was worth it.

———

The next morning, campus felt different. Eyes lingered a second too long. Two girls in the art building whispered something about Norman Marcus when I walked by. So. Word had gotten out. I doubted the Outlaws said anything, but Logan wasn't exactly quiet, and it wasn't like I was difficult to identify. The whole student body was buzzing about Logan and his team-mates showing up at the breakfast, and the artists were just as star struck as I had been by Norman. Unlike Logan Kemp, I didn't enjoy the extra attention.

After my first class, I went to the Remembrance Day cere-mony on the main quad. Students and faculty stood in a loose semi-circle around the cenotaph. Someone from Political Science read *In Flanders Fields*. A trumpet played the Last Post, thin and slightly sharp in the wind. Students from ROTC laid wreaths and we shared our two minutes of silence.

I stared at the stone, at the dates carved into it, at the tiny poppies pinned to all our coats. Men my age, younger. Boys who'd left school and never come back. My anxieties about school and jobs and even Logan shrank under the weight of it.

When I got home, the answering machine's little red light was blinking like a distress beacon. I hit Play.

"Hi, sweetheart," my mom's voice chirped. "We saw the

paper. Your father nearly choked on his toast. Are you really dating someone on the Blizzard? Call me. Love you."

I thunked my forehead against the wall.

———

My drive to the warehouse on Wednesday was uneventful, but my arrival was cause for celebration because the only vehicles in the lot were Norman's Volvo and a delivery van.

For the first hour, I worked in blessed silence. Inventorying hardware. Sorting artist submissions into stacks. Drafting a preliminary student outreach sheet Norman had asked for.

No Logan.

By lunchtime, the knot in my chest had loosened a fraction. By three, it had morphed into something new: guilt. Maybe I should've called him. I thought back over our conversations and realized he was right. I hadn't explicitly spelled out my concerns, thinking they were obvious. He'd admitted to missing the team and his friends. It was *his* choices that led to that gap. It seemed obvious that I wouldn't want to be seen as accepting his behavior.

But, things had changed a lot since that first night in the grocery store. I should've been more open with him.

At five, Norman poked his head into the little office nook where I'd spread out submissions. "Go home, Crystal," he said. "You're making the rest of us look bad."

"I still have to type up the draft for—"

"Tomorrow." He tapped his fingers on the now actual door frame for his office.

Though I knew he wasn't going to take his own advice, I packed my bag, shrugged into my coat, and headed out. The lot had emptied down to Jenna's little car and Norman's Volvo.

I slid into the driver's seat, turned the key, and—

Nothing.

Well, not nothing. A sad cough. A weak whine. Then nothing.

"Don't do this to me," I whispered, trying again. The engine made a noise like a dying blender and gave up.

Shit. I hadn't done anything, had I? Hit anything?

I tried one more time. The car responded by flickering the dash lights once, then going dark.

"Cool," I groaned, dropping my head to the steering wheel. "Love that."

I looked up at the dark warehouse. The light was already drained from the sky, and it suddenly felt a lot creepier being alone here in the parking lot.

I scrambled out of the car, locked it, and hustled back inside. Norman was at the far end of the space, taking measurements. He turned as I approached. "Forget something?"

"My car won't start," I said, a little breathless.

He waved a hand. "I was just talking to Logan about the reception. You can call him back in the office."

I blinked. Obviously. That's what boyfriends were for.

CHAPTER
Fourteen

NORMAN STOOD in his office and watched while I dialled Logan's number, making it impossible to call my dad instead.

Logan answered on the second ring, short of breath. "Yeah?"

My mind was instantly doing somersaults. Was he working out? Was he—?

"Hey, it's me."

Pause. "Hey." The TV echoed in the background. Okay, so he probably didn't have company over then?

"Um, I'm at the gallery and my car—well, Jenna's car—isn't starting." I glanced up. Norman was organizing something on a bookshelf that was new since the last time I was here.

"Is someone there with you?"

"Yeah. Norman M—Mr. Marcus is here." Damn it. I couldn't say his full name with him standing right in front of me.

Logan huffed a small laugh. "I just got home from practice. Let me grab keys. I'll be there in fifteen."

"You don't have to—" I started, but he cut me off.

"Crystal. I'm coming."

I exhaled. "Okay. Thanks." Besides the fifteen minute guessti-mate he gave, I had no idea where he lived. The only thing I did know was that his house was big enough to host a party.

I replaced the handset.

Norman turned to face me. "You can call me Norman, you know."

I didn't know what to say to that. "I didn't want to be disrespectful."

He looked amused. "All sorted?"

"Logan's coming." I hoped my cheeks didn't look as hot as they felt. I hated inconveniencing anyone, and I had no idea what to do about Jenna's car. Was the battery just dead? Maybe Logan had cables and we could jump it?

Norman nodded. "Good. Come here. Let me show you something while you wait."

He led me to one of the folding tables near the back wall, currently buried under a small avalanche of portfolios. Thick binders, battered black cases, manila envelopes. He spread his hands over the mess. "You're interested in curating."

It was a statement, not a question. "Yes. Absolutely."

"Well, these are submissions for the opening. Student work, upcoming artists. Some promising, I think. Obviously I already have our main attractions targeted." He flipped open a binder on top and handed it to me. "What do you see?"

The binder belonged to a sculptor from Lethbridge. Steel, stone, a lot of angst. I stared at the pictures for a long moment. "Strong material sense," I said slowly. "But it's all . . . I don't know. It feels a little performative. I don't know if that's the right word. Like he's making them for people to display at the top of their driveway to feel fancy."

His mouth curved. He took the binder back and shut it, then pulled out the next. "And this one?"

We went through a few more. A painter from Saskatoon obsessed with empty interiors, a printmaker who used wheat as a recurring motif, a photographer who played with overexposure. I gave gut reactions. What else could I do? I had zero information on these people. Norman pushed back on some, but most of the time he was quiet which was actually so much worse.

After a while, he nodded. "You have a good eye. Instincts will sharpen with time, but they're sound. I'd like you to talk to someone." Norman began restacking the binders and folders. "Her name is Alison Kerr. She's an associate curator at the Glenbow. Brilliant, a little intimidating, excellent at her job. She consults on some of our programming. When we go to the Palliser, I'd like you to meet her. It's a little selfish, though. She's always complaining there's no one in Calgary under forty who understands both practice and theory. I'd like to prove her wrong."

My stomach flipped. "I don't know—"

"You don't have to impress her, my recommendation alone will do that. I only want the two of you to be connected."

It felt like I might physically levitate. I swallowed hard. "That would be amazing. Thank you."

"Good." He closed another portfolio just as I heard the familiar rumble of a truck outside, then the slam of a door. A moment later, footsteps echoed in the empty building.

"Honey, I'm home!" Logan called out.

Hilarious. I rolled my eyes.

Norman's mouth tipped up. "It seems your chariot awaits."

I scooped up my bag and thanked him as he assured me it was fine to leave my car there overnight if needed.

Logan stood just inside the front doors, cheeks pink from the cold. He was in grey sweatpants, Adidas slides, and a hoodie. His hair was mussed, like it had just dried after a shower. He looked relaxed. A little sleepy maybe? Completely the opposite of his suit on campus, and it was disarming.

He held up his keys. "Heard someone needed a tow fairy."

I stopped in front of him. "I really appreciate you coming."

"I live less than ten minutes from here. Not a big deal."

We walked out together. The temperature had dropped, and Jenna's car sat sadly in the lot, a little blue lump under a fresh dusting of snow.

Logan headed straight for it, rubbing his hands together like he'd been waiting for this moment. "Alright. Pop the hood."

I walked to the driver's side door and opened it, searching for any kind of lever. I'd seen my dad pop his hood before but had no idea how to do it. Finally I gave up. "I don't know how to do that. Don't mock me."

His mouth quirked. "You think I'd mock you?"

"I know you would."

He grinned. "Driver's side. Down by your knee."

I bent over and searched. Sure enough. The hood thunked open with a sad little groan.

Logan propped it up and leaned in. "Battery terminal's loose," he murmured. "But I don't see anything else obvious."

I stood beside him and took in the car innards. "Hm. Yeah. Me either."

Logan bit back a smile. "Okay, princess. Let's jump her."

"There it is."

He laughed. "What? It was a joke." He jogged to his truck to grab jumper cables. When he returned, he clipped the red side onto the port on my battery, then popped his own hood and connected both cables there. He ran back and clipped the black side to something under my hood that wasn't the battery.

"Are they on right?" My dad said something about electrocution or sudden death when he was giving me and my brother the run down on car maintenance. Clearly that stuck. And nothing else.

Logan gave me a look. "Yeah." He walked back to the truck and started his engine.

I jumped, expecting it to spark or blow up. One of the two.

"Get in and try it," Logan called from the front seat.

I got in, turned the key, and the engine roared to life. I laughed out loud, my face lighting up like a Christmas tree. Logan was out, standing in front of the car again.

"It worked!" I went to hop out, but Logan motioned for me to stay.

"Keep it running. Let the battery charge."

I nodded, hands gripping the wheel as cold air blasted from the vents. I flicked off the heater until the engine had time to warm up. Logan disconnected the cables, tossed them in the back of his truck, and tapped the hood twice before meeting me at the window.

"If you drive it straight home, you should be fine."

"Should?" I repeated. Not the vote of confidence I was looking for.

He laughed at the expression on my face. "I'll follow you."

He looked *good* in those sweats. And there was something about him knowing exactly what to do, bossing me around with all that confidence . . .

I forced my eyes down to the dashboard. Yikes. Maybe I didn't need the heater after all.

When Logan's truck lights flicked on, I pulled out of the lot. Everything went swimmingly until about three blocks away, when the wheel suddenly wouldn't turn. The dashboard lights flickered like dying fireflies, and the engine stopped. No response when I pressed on the gas.

"No, no, no!" I coasted hopelessly toward the edge of the road like a grocery cart.

Logan pulled over behind me and parked on the curb. He jogged up to me, breath clouding in the freezing air. "Died?"

I couldn't roll down the window, so I opened the door. "Do you think we didn't run it long enough?"

"I'm guessing it's the alternator. Probably why it died in the first place."

He may as well have been speaking Mandarin. "Okay. So . . . " My brain spun. There was a gas station on the corner. We could call a tow truck, but I had no idea how much that would cost this time of night.

Logan reached in and pulled the lever to pop the hood. His arm grazed my thigh on the way up, and I sucked in a breath.

"I'll jump it one more time. If we're lucky, it'll run long enough to get it to my place."

"Your place?"

"Yeah. We can park it there, and tomorrow you can call a tow without freezing or getting murdered."

I nodded. "I do love not getting murdered." It was downtown Calgary. Not exactly Los Angeles, but still. I didn't want to leave Jenna's car here on a random street. Or even in the gallery parking lot.

Logan pulled up, turned on his hazards, and connected the cables again. When it was up and running he said, "Follow me. Don't stop. Not at lights, not for pedestrians."

"Right. Run the children over."

Logan laughed, took his cables back, and pulled out. I tried not to stop, following him through yellow lights, one that was definitely red. But by sheer force of Logan's will, divine luck, or both, the engine lasted until Logan pulled into a driveway five minutes or so later. The steering locked up right as I turned in, and Logan had to give it a push to get it fully off the street.

I put on the emergency brake and got out, sagging against the frame. "How much are alternators?"

He shoved his hands in his pockets. "Not cheap."

I groaned.

"But it's not your car, right?"

"I feel like I'm responsible."

He shook his head. "It's a car part. It happens." He scuffed a sandaled foot on the driveway. "I'll drive you home, but do you mind if I eat first?"

"You haven't eaten?"

"No, my food arrived right when you called."

I processed that sentence. Logan left to come help me with the car when he'd ordered food in and it was hot and ready? I looked down at my wrist, but I wasn't wearing my watch. "It's been, like, an hour." I met his eyes, horrified. "Logan, I could've waited."

He waved me off. "It's fine."

"Not fine!"

He ran a hand through his hair, then turned back to his garage. "It's fine, Crys. Just come inside so my stomach doesn't eat itself."

Fifteen

LOGAN CLOSED THE GARAGE DOOR, and I followed him up the narrow staircase from the garage to his condo. Hardwood steps. Nice. The building itself was modern and new, the facade in red brick and white trim.

When he pushed open the door at the top, I placed my shoes on the mat and took in the kitchen and living area. It was simple and minimalist. Light wood and chrome accents with a wide open living space flanked by big windows overlooking the street. There was a low-profile grey sofa, glass coffee table, geometric rug, and a large-screen TV.

Logan tossed his keys into the ceramic dish by the door and headed straight for the counter. "It might still be warm." He flipped open a container of shawarma and pulled two plates from the cupboard. "Want to dish up?"

I wandered onto the tile. "It's your food, Logan—"

"I always order too much."

Truthfully, the scent of roasted meet and warm spices was making me salivate. How long ago did I eat lunch? I wasn't strong enough to say no. "Sure. I'll have a little."

Logan pushed the takeout container and a fork toward me. I

scooped out a reasonable portion, then he added another scoop on top despite my protests.

"Want to heat it up?"

I took a small bite. It wasn't hot by any means, but it wasn't cold. "No, I'm good."

He scooped the rest onto his plate and popped it in the microwave. "I like my food cold or hot. Nothing in between."

"Hm. Why does that not surprise me?" I sat on one of the stools at the island.

He pressed his palms into the counter across from me. "What does that mean?"

"It means you like things a certain way. And you usually get it."

"Yeah?" He raised an eyebrow.

"Don't—" I waved my fork at him. "Be all flirty right now. I'm still mad at you." I stabbed a potato with my fork. It was somehow still crispy on the outside, soft inside. Perfection despite the room temperature.

"Impossible." The microwave beeped and he took his food out. "I save your life, give you food, and you can't get over one comment?"

I smirked. "Well, that one comment did make it so I can't have sex until January, so . . ." Logan laughed out loud, stirring his food around. I grimaced. "What are you doing?"

"Making perfect bites." When my brows pinched further, he shifted closer and showed me his plate. "You need a bite of everything in every forkful. Feta, hummus, olives, potatoes. Easier if you mix it together first."

"I can do that by just grabbing each thing one at a time." I demonstrated, filling the tines. "Then it doesn't look like dog vomit."

Logan filled his fork with hummus colored everything and shoved it in his mouth with a groan that was borderline obscene.

I snorted.

He chewed and swallowed, then moved to sit on the stool next to me. "I'm sorry about the breakfast, by the way. Not totally sorry I said what I did, but I should've talked to you first."

I gave him side eye. "Not sorry you said it?"

He shook his head. "That guy, Jake? He was looking at you like—" he took a bite. "He was undressing you with his eyes."

I swivelled to face him. "Maybe that's what I'm into."

Logan pulled his face into what I can only assume was a smolder. "Mm. Crystal. Remember the cafeteria? When I couldn't even find a romantic place to stick my tongue in your mouth?"

I smacked his shoulder, nearly choking on my slow-roasted lamb. "It wasn't romantic, okay? But it was *hot*. We were making out on school property after hours—"

"So that's your thing? Exciting and forbidden?"

My cheeks flushed. "I think for it to be a 'thing,' it has to happen more than once."

He took another bite, raising an eyebrow. "It only happened once?"

"Well, yeah. He was in town for the tournament."

"There's more than one day at a tournament. It's pretty easy to figure out how to do it *more than once*."

The humor in the situation circled and disappeared down the drain. I held back the dig sitting on the tip of my tongue. "Yeah. I guess so."

We ate in silence a moment, then Logan let out a long breath. "Sorry. Word vomit."

I pursed my lips. He wasn't wrong.

Logan lowered his voice. "I think if I'm being honest, it wasn't just you I was defending at the breakfast." He scooped up another bite onto his fork, but didn't eat it. "It's not easy to see the team without me on it."

That was exactly it. The look in his eyes that morning? It was the same look I'd seen on his face, on Rob's, Axel's, and Rory's right before they battled it out in the last period on the ice. That same image of a warrior curling around his family flashed in my head.

I finished chewing, then rested my elbow on the counter, turning to face him. "They're still your team, Logan."

He made a noise in his throat. "Yeah, well, I don't know if they want me anymore." His lashes brushed his cheeks as he lowered his head, scooping up a stray chickpea from the counter.

I focused hard on my own plate. When he got like this, all broody, like a thundercloud rolling in on the horizon, my body perked up like a lightning rod. Maybe I did have a thing for exciting and forbidden?

Hockey. We were talking about hockey. "They might not want you for the same things. But you know every guy there wishes he was in your shoes. You're not on the ice with them, but they're all watching you."

"That's what I'm afraid of." He took his last bite and stood, his stool scraping against the tile. "I shouldn't be anyone's role model."

I finished my food and followed him to the sink. "What's more compelling than someone who screws up and figures it out? You and Rob seemed pretty normal today."

He nodded, rinsing his plate. "Better, at least."

I waited in line for the sink, but when he turned, I froze. "Are you—?" I set my plate down and turned his chin to the side to get a better look. "Oh, it's a pepper." I laughed.

"What is?" He tried to look, but I held his face while I grabbed a napkin.

"I thought you were bleeding, but it's just a piece of—" I swiped it off his cheek. "There, see?" I dropped my hand from his chin and showed him.

When his hand cupped mine to bring the napkin higher so he could see it, I realized how close I'd stepped. The heat from his body diffused into mine as my skin buzzed under his fingertips.

He frowned. "Huh. That does look like blood." The warm kitchen light fell across his hair and skin, making all of it glow golden. He glanced up, his eyes meeting mine, then flicking to my mouth.

The storm clouds were fully overhead, and the hairs on the back of my neck stood on end.

His fingers shifted, lighting up the back of my hand as he drew a breath, slow and shaky. My hands started to tingle. My pulse thudded in my ears.

Logan moved toward me, and when my heart felt like it was attached to the other end of his jumper cables, a crash made me jump out of my skin.

"Shit." Logan dropped my hand and peered into the sink. My plate. He'd knocked it off the edge of the counter where I'd set it.

"Sorry, I shouldn't have—"

"No, it's not broken." His breathing was shallow and quick.

I stepped back, searching for the trash. There was a bin at the end of the island, so I beelined for it and tossed the napkin. "I should—"

"Yeah," he jumped in, rubbing the back of his neck. "I should take you home."

"Right." I turned in a half circle, then pointed at my shoes. "Thank you so much for dinner."

"Oh, no problem."

"And for saving my life." I shot him a cheesy smile.

He huffed a laugh and snagged his keys from the bowl. "Uh, also my pleasure."

I lost my balance and slammed a hand into the wall to keep from falling over. "Sorry."

"Do you want to use the bench?" He pointed at the seat by the coat closet.

"No, I'm good. Just—it's late, I guess." I shoved my second foot into my shoe. "There. Okay. Ready."

Logan nodded to the door. "After you."

I DISCOVERED two things about Jenna the next day. One, her brother was a mechanic, and two, her brother's shop was only a few streets over from Logan's condo. He sent a tow truck over first thing, which left me free to make my weekly sojourn to Rob and Shar's.

It didn't disappoint. Carter was warm and heavy in my arms. He made a tiny sighing noise, scrunched his face, then melted against my chest like I was the safest thing in the world. His hair was soft, downy fuzz that made my heart do a ridiculous *boop* every time I looked at him.

Shar flopped onto the couch beside me with the energy of someone who hadn't slept since the Trudeau years. "He likes you." She stretched her legs out and wiggled her toes. "How are you enjoying being a certified aunt?"

"I kind of expected a badge. Or a tiara. Maybe a pin?"

"No pins around babies," she said automatically, then snorted. "Listen to me. I'm one week postpartum and already thinking about safety hazards. Do you know how many outlets are in this house?"

I glanced around the living room, but didn't see plug-ins. Instead, my eyes caught on the laundry basket overflowing with tiny onesies and cotton blankets, a half-packed diaper bag by the door, and the textbooks stacked on the coffee table. "This is insane, Shar. I have no idea how you're functioning."

Shar leaned her head back and closed her eyes. "Honestly, neither do I. My boobs finally don't feel like they're about to explode, though, so that's something."

"Carter, did you figure out breastfeeding?" I cooed. A sentence I never in a thousand years thought I'd say before I graduated.

Shar shifted, adjusting the pillow behind her back. "Oh, he didn't have a choice. Stubborn little bug."

I laughed, brushing a finger over Carter's impossibly tiny hand. "He is stupid cute."

"He is." She beamed at us. "Rob cries like twice a day while looking at him. Don't tell him I told you."

I mimed zipping up my lips, but my heart melted at that. Of course he did. I never would've guessed, but Rob Thompson, with all his rough edges, was gooey in the middle.

Shar sighed. "I'm just trying to keep up with everything. We both are. My professors are being saints, but I still have performances coming up, and rehearsals, and pumping between classes. It's a circus."

"You're a saint."

"I'm—" she yawned, rubbing her eyes. "Surviving. So that's something."

I breathed in a full whiff of intoxicating baby smell. "You're keeping a tiny human alive."

At that, Carter let out a little "ehh" noise that made us both "awww!" Shar reached over and brushed his cheek.

"Okay, Chunk," she murmured. "Sleep a little longer. It's not snack time yet."

We sat there for a moment, just being. Somehow, at home I was always antsy, but I could've sat there for hours without moving once.

Shar crossed her legs under her. "So? Any updates for me?"

I tensed, and Carter's golden brow furrowed. "Not really. Everything's fine. I've been doing more admin work at the gallery, so that's great." Where would I even start with the last week? Everything I'd updated her on had to do with the one person I had zero interest in bringing up at this moment.

Her eyebrow arched. "Crystal."

"Shar."

She gave me a look, and I gave her a look back, but she already had that mom energy. She won, no contest.

"Fine," I sighed. "It's complicated."

"In what way?"

"Well I'm sure Rob filled you in on what he did at the breakfast."

She smirked. "Oh he definitely did. Classic Logan."

"Really?"

"Yeah, he's all fun and games until someone threatens him or someone he cares about. Once tried to fight a guy in Red Deer because the guy threw a pretzel at Axel. Ooh, and Jake is pissed, by the way. Have you not talked with him since?"

I frowned. Huh. I guess I hadn't. It took me a moment to respond because I was still hung up on what she'd just said. *Someone he cares about?* "I didn't think Jake would want to talk to me. He thinks I'm with Logan."

She shrugged. "You could still keep your options open. Doesn't this whole agreement end in December?" I nodded, and she grinned mischievously. "It'll definitely ramp up the tension."

I shook my head. "I thought you were a wholesome wife and mother now?"

Shar laughed. "C'mon, I have to live vicariously through you a little. Speaking of which, don't you have a fancy event coming up?"

I lit up. "The Palliser. I have no idea what I'm going to wear."

Shar jumped up from the couch with an impressive amount of energy for someone running on less than four hours of sleep every night. "I have the perfect thing."

She appeared a few seconds later with a straight black off-the-shoulder cocktail dress. "I got it for our quick honeymoon weekend and didn't get a chance to wear it."

I shook my head. "I'm not going to wear your dress first!"

"Babe, it'll be a solid six months before I can fit into this again. Please. Wear the hell out of it." She draped it over the arm of the couch by my purse and shoes.

Carter seemed to sense his mom's arrival because he started to squirm. Shar sat beside me and reached for him.

"I'll go so you can feed him."

She made a face. "I'd tell you to stay but it's still easiest for me to do this topless."

"Ugh, you're going to make me miss a free boob flash?"

She chortled. "Anytime for you. They are pretty fantastic right now." I laughed as she turned to the side, showing me her full D cups.

"Jealous." I leaned over and gave her a hug, careful not to squish Carter, or her boobs, between us.

She pulled back. "See you tomorrow?"

"You know it."

———

The Outlaws played at home the next night and Chase was with the Hitmen, so Maddie and I finally had a date. It was a packed crowd and the air buzzed with the kind of electricity that only university hockey could generate. Shar arrived ten minutes after puck drop, and Carter was wrapped in so many layers he looked like a marshmallow with eyes. Every female in the bleachers struggled to watch the actual game, they were so distracted by his cuteness.

Really, who could blame them? The chances of seeing a baby on campus were lower than spotting a moose.

Shar soaked in every compliment while Maddie and I helped her juggle the diaper bag, the baby, the blanket, and the bottle. It was Carter's first real outing, and we came prepared to help our girl.

But once Carter was settled in for a nap and we were midway through the first period, it felt exactly like before. Back when it was just us. I let that wash over me like a warm hug.

Of course, I thought of Logan. Remembering how he used to play—how he still played. I'd been watching his games, and he was getting an impressive number of shifts as a rookie. He still had that same explosive energy, those smooth transitions. I could spot when he got the puck before I even saw the number on his jersey.

"I don't understand how Rob is playing better," Maddie called out after he sprawled on the ice to tap a pass to Axel for our first goal. "His reaction time should be terrible with the late nights he's pulling."

Shar leaned her head on my shoulder. "He's exhausted, but he's the happiest he's ever been. His words, not mine."

Ugh. The cuteness was going to kill me.

We watched the game in a blur of snacks, baby passing, and cheers, especially when Rory scored a shorthanded beauty and Rob got a breakaway for a goal in the third. By the end of the game, an Outlaws win, the three of us were borderline feral with nostalgia.

"Ranchman's?" Maddie raised a brow.

"Like you even have to ask."

———

Ranchman's was already humming when Maddie and I walked in. We'd stayed longer at the Douglas Dome to help Sharla get Carter in his carseat. She opted to get him home for the night, and I said a silent prayer that Carter, after all the excitement, would sack out for at least four hours in a stretch this time.

I didn't know I'd missed the smell of wings, spilled beer, and shower gel but I was breathing it in like I was at a rose garden. We pushed through the crowd to see our table at the back was already half-filled.

Axel stood when he saw us. "LADIES!" he boomed, arms wide like we were returning soldiers.

Rory gestured at the empty stools. "Spill the tea, MacMillan."

I laughed. "What tea? I have no tea!"

Axel shoved a plate of nachos toward me. I spotted Jake a few seats down. "We need insider information!"

"Are we insiders?" Maddie snorted as she slid onto a stool.

"Crystal is," Rory said. "Kemp's been on every news outlet in this city over the past week. Did you see his goal against the Canucks?"

Oh, I'd seen it. Jenna may have recorded the game on our VCR, and I'd rewatched that particular section enough times to see scratches on the tape.

I groaned internally. "Sounds like you know as much as I do!" I shouted over the music.

"I would ask about his dick, but I've already seen it." Axel grinned, shoving a chip in his mouth.

I rolled my eyes. "See? I have nothing to add."

"Kay, if you're not going to give us details, can you at least get us tickets?" Rory leaned his elbows on the table, smirking. Jake tuned in at that question.

"I want the Oilers game Thursday." Axel waggled his eyebrow. "Come on, Crystal. I know you have it in you." Laughter and post-game chatter swelled around us, and it almost made me tear up. I knew I'd missed it, but I didn't realize how much it would feel like home.

"You're asking me to manipulate my boyfriend for you?" I teased. The 'B' word felt strange on my tongue, but it didn't feel wrong. That made me pause.

Axel's hand flew to his heart. "We would never."

"Tell Logan I'm offering sexual favors." Rory poured himself another beer.

I winked. "I'm sure he'll be tempted."

"Ooh! Maddie! Forgot to tell you, I had this math midterm . . ." Axel jumped into a discussion on proofs and equations that my brain was too distracted to follow after hearing 'sex' and 'Logan' in the same sentence.

That moment at his house replayed in my head every hour, and I needed to make it stop. No amount of rationalizing was working.

"Hey." Jake left his stool to stand with us. He rocked on his feet a moment, then said, "I'm sorry if I caused a problem the other day. I didn't know about Kemp."

I waved him off, my nerves jumping. "You're fine. He took it a little too seriously."

Jake nodded. "How long have you two, uh, you know. Been together?"

"Not long," I answered, regretting it when his eyebrow jumped.

"Is it serious?"

A pit yawned open beneath my ribs. All that defensiveness I saw in Logan the other day poured into me at full force. Was he really asking that when he'd been told point blank I had a boyfriend? Maybe Logan's assessment of him had been spot on. "I think so, yeah," I said with an exaggerated smile. "I guess time will tell."

I turned back to the nachos, giving Maddie a look. I was not telling Logan about this.

Jake thankfully wandered back to his seat, and Maddie and I stayed until Chase called the bar and told her he was on his way home. She dropped me off on the way.

When I walked in with my skin humming and ears ringing, the apartment was quiet. Jenna and Lindsey were either out or already asleep.

I dropped my coat on a chair, kicked off my boots, and headed straight for the phone.

Logan answered on the first ring. "Hey. How was the game?"

"Amazing. You should've seen Rob's goal . . ." I gave him a recap with special attention on my preferred highlights, ending with our night at Ranchman's. Minus my short conversation with number twelve.

At one point I paused to get a blanket from the couch. We really needed to invest in a phone with a longer cord.

"How was practice?" I asked after my monologue.

Logan grunted. "We have a new conditioning coach. He's brutal. I'm not sure if my legs followed me home."

I frowned. "Is that normal? To push that hard right before a game?"

"Crys, it's the NHL. I'm getting paid a shit-ton of money. I don't think they care if my quads are tired."

I bristled. "Well they should care. How can you perform your best if they're grinding you like that?"

Logan chuckled. "Okay, I kind of like this feisty side of you."

I ignored his attempt to pivot. "Are you still working with that nutritionist?"

His grin was audible. "I'm eating, MacMillan. I promise. We have meals after practice. Lots of chicken. Rice. Protein shakes. I even eat the greens."

"Okay. Good." I drew a breath, trying to reign in whatever weird mama bear moment I was having. But seriously, how did they expect these guys to perform at peak levels when they were running them into the ground? Logan was one of the hardest workers I knew on the ice. He and Rob were always out there after hours, and I had no doubt he was doing the same thing with the Blizzard. If he said he was hurting, it was ten times worse than what he was letting on.

"Thanks for being a good fake girlfriend."

I scoffed. "I'm the best fake girlfriend. Oh, get this. Forgot to tell you, at Ranchman's, Rory and Axel were asking for tickets—"

"To what?"

"The game you have against the Oilers. I told them—"

"They want to come?"

"Yeah, Logan, they want to come. They were using me to get to you, and I said—"

"I can definitely get them tickets."

I frowned. "You're kind of killing the punchline of my story. Where I tell you I set proper expectations. That they can't expect me to milk this connection all the time."

He chuckled. "You can milk it all you want."

"Oh, for the love. I'm going to bed. Good—"

"No! No, I'm sorry. I promise, I'll behave. But seriously, I can get them tickets. I haven't used my freebies."

I pursed my lips. "Well, you can't just give it to them. You have to make them earn it."

Logan considered that for a moment. "Yeah. Okay, I've got it. I'll email them."

"What is it?"

"Afraid you're not privy to that information. I'll tell you before the game, though."

"Logan—"

"Do you want to come?"

My heart skipped. "Of course I want to come."

He sucked in a breath. "You've never asked me, so I didn't know—"

"Logan, I didn't want to use you for tickets." I heard the grin before he opened his mouth, and cut him off. "No, don't say it."

He guffawed. "I think you'll like it."

"I won't."

"It's a good one. C'mon—"

"I'm going to bed—

"What do you want to use me for?" He blurted, and I couldn't help but laugh.

"Goodnight, Logan."

"No, you hang up."

"I'm not—"

"I know, I want to talk longer, too!"

"GOODNIGHT, LOGAN."

His laugh was contagious. "Goodnight, Crys."

I hung up and walked to my room with a stupid grin still on my face.

CHAPTER
Seventeen

ON THURSDAY, I woke to someone pounding on my door like they were trying to escape a burning building. I groaned, facedown on my pillow, throat dry, brain foggy. I searched for a glimpse of my clock. *Who in their right mind knocked at 7:12 a.m.?*

Jenna yelled something murderous from her room.

The knocking came again. Louder.

I threw on a hoodie that may or may not have been clean, and padded down the hall in my short shorts.

"Who is it?" I called, voice scratchy.

"It's Axel!"

Of course it was.

I opened the door, and there he stood. Fifteen pounds of enthusiasm packed into 210 pounds of actual muscle, wearing a too-thin jacket, beanie askew, and holding a coffee cup.

"Morning, Mac! I brought you breakfast."

I blinked at him. "Why?"

He pushed the coffee into my hands. "Don't ask questions you don't want the answers to."

"No, I absolutely want the answers. I—"

Before I could finish that fever dream of a sentence, he lifted a paper bag from under his arm and thrust it toward me. "Sandwich. Hash browns. A donut because sugar."

I opened my mouth to say something else, but he was already jogging down the walkway.

The day only got weirder from there. Between classes, I was heading through the arts courtyard when Bear intercepted me like a bearded heat-seeking missile.

"Crys," he rumbled.

"Bear," I answered with a healthy amount of skepticism.

He thrust another cup toward me. "Steamer. Peppermint."

"Okay, what the hell is—"

"Have a great day!" Then he walked away very quickly, which Bear never does. Bear moves like a glacier unless food is involved.

At lunch, I walked into the Douglas café, fully planning to grab soup and sprint to class, when Rory popped up in front of me like a jack-in-the-box.

"Hey! I'm buying you lunch today."

I crossed my arms. "No you're not. Not unless you tell me what's going on."

He scoffed, the picture of innocence. "Can't we show a little love to one of our biggest fans?"

I stared him down. "Rory."

He mirrored my pose. "Crystal. You can tell me what you want or I'll order you my favourite."

"Which is?"

"Burger. Four patties."

I pursed my lips. "Fine. Panini."

"Got it. And a cookie!"

The final straw came after my last class. I was packing my bag when the classroom door swung open and in walked Nick. Holding flowers.

"For you," he said brightly.

I threw out my hands. "Okay, seriously. Is someone dead?"

Nick laughed, handing me the bouquet. "Nope. See you tonight. You're coming to the game, right?"

"Yep, I'm—" I froze.

Well, you can't just give it to them. You have to make them earn it.

Okay, I've got it. I'll email them.

Logan frigging Kemp.

LOGAN HADN'T JUST GOTTEN us tickets. He'd gone full fairy godmother.

We didn't realize it until we got to the Saddledome and the usher didn't steer us toward the nosebleeds or the student-discount section, but up. Up the escalator, down a private hallway with framed jerseys and corporate logos, and straight into a glass-fronted luxury suite.

"Holy…" Rory stopped dead in the doorway. "We're not supposed to be in here."

"We're ABSOLUTELY supposed to be in here," Axel said, barging past him. "Look at this. There's shrimp. And, holy shit, is that a meat carving station?"

It was. There was an entire table laid out with hot food. Sliders, wings, nachos, pasta, three different dips I couldn't identify but was likely to bathe in. The other side was full of veggies, chips and candy, and had a cooler built into the counter that held more pop than a 7-Eleven. There was a private bathroom off to the side, and big leather seats faced the ice in a row with a little ledge for plates and drinks.

"Crystal," Maddie whispered, her eyes wide. "What did you *do*?"

"Her favours are better than mine!" Axel crowed, and Maddie smacked him for me.

Chase and Rob were already digging into the food behind Nick and Bear while Shar arranged Carter's carrier beside one of the leather seats and tucked a blanket around him. The baby blinked sleepily, thoroughly unimpressed by his first NHL experience.

An attendant popped her head in. "Hi there, everyone—I'm Kelly. If you need anything, let me know. The food's all yours, bar tab is covered, and we'll replenish between periods."

Axel stared at her like she'd just announced free tuition. "Hell, yes!"

When all the guys were stocked with food and drinks, we settled in and watched the players pour onto the ice for warmup. The crowd noise swelled, and as people stood I noticed a few people wearing Logan's jersey.

For some reason, that kicked me in the gut. This was real. Logan was an NHL player. He'd made it all the way. It was one thing to see these guys on the ice on TV and another to have watched someone make their career happen right before your eyes.

Rory nudged me with his elbow. "This is wild."

He was telling me.

Down on the ice, Logan skated a few hard laps, stretching out his stride, easy and smooth. He looked good. Loose, focused. He stopped at the blue line and dropped to the ice, spreading his knees wide and . . . holy hell. That was the stretch of all stretches.

The guys lost it. Cat calling and screaming Logan's name.

"You know he's doing that for us!" Axel slapped his knee.

I shook my head at Shar and Maddie. Rob pretended to be mature, but his eyes were starting to water, he was fighting a laugh so hard.

The lights dimmed, and the anthem singer came out. We all stood. I balanced my plate on the ledge, pressed one hand to the poppy still on my coat while the players lined up on the blue line with their helmets off, heads bowed.

When the opening faceoff dropped, the crowd went wild. Our group whooped and hollered when Logan appeared in the third shift.

"Look at his gap control," Chase murmured. "He's playing deeper. Smarter."

Maddie nodded, completely in the zone. I didn't know what all that meant, but I couldn't keep my eyes off Logan. No matter where the puck was, he was at the center of my vision.

Thirty seconds in, the other team chipped the puck out sloppily and tried to break out. Logan intercepted the pass at centre, pivoted hard, and without even looking, sent a perfect, saucered backhand to Rourke. Glove save ended the play but damn if that wasn't impressive.

Later in the period, Logan was on the penalty kill for nearly forty seconds. Twice he poked pucks off sticks and then got a solid clear to earn the whole group a break.

Midway through the second, tied 1–1, Logan picked up speed through the neutral zone, took a pass just over the red line, and bulldozed past one defender at the blue line with a nasty little inside-out deke. The second defender tried to angle him off, but Logan lowered his shoulder, protected the puck with his hip, and one-handed the puck across the crease to his teammate, who flicked it up over the goalie pads for a 2-1 lead.

Our suite went berserk.

I stared down at Logan as he went to the bench, tapping gloves with his teammates. I was on the phone with him last night. Every night this week actually. He was just a guy, but seeing him down there . . . It sparked something in my chest.

"That's our boy!" Axel crowed.

I wanted to record every second of our suite experience for Logan so he could watch it later.

By the third period, the score hadn't changed, and we were

all on the edges of our seats when one of the Blizzard got a penalty for tripping.

"There he is!" Bear called as Logan came on the ice.

"They're going to put him on the kill every game," Chase said. "He reads it so well."

I leaned into Shar. "You okay?" It was one thing to talk about Logan every once in a while. Another to have him dominate the conversation for the night.

She smiled at me. "So good. I'm really proud of him. He's worked so hard for this."

Rob slung an arm over her shoulder, pulling her close.

Okay. So they were better humans than I'd ever be. But I'd known that since the second Rob got up in front of the entire student body and proposed.

Still, a sliver of guilt wedged between my ribs. Shar was fine with all of this now because it was fun and games. But what if it were real? What if something did happen between me and Logan? Would she be fine with it then?

I banished the thought from my mind. Not something I needed to worry about because Logan and I were supposed to be just friends. Full stop.

I turned my attention fully to the game, and when the Blizzard won 3-1, I nearly screamed myself hoarse.

Logan got two assists and was named first star. When he skated out for the little lap, helmet off, hair damp, his name and stats on the Jumbotron, the crowd roared.

Axel scoffed. "He needs to stop showing off."

After the post-game milling-around, we filed out of the suite. Kelly thanked us, we thanked her back, then apologized when Axel lifted her off the ground in a hug, and followed another staff member down to the player's area.

Logan came through the doors into the tunnel with Rourke and a couple other guys, hair damp, black dress pants and a fitted long-sleeve shirt. He spotted us instantly. Hard to miss a group that included half the Outlaws and one baby held up like Simba wearing your team's onesie.

He grinned. "Nice digs, eh?"

The guys mauled him. All I heard was "Best food of my life!" and "You took the ice's virginity!"

But when Rob stepped forward with Carter, the entire hallway quieted.

"Good game, bud." Rob said.

Logan seemed at a loss for words as he crouched and touched Carter's hand. "Can't believe this. He's so cute."

"Do you want to hold him?"

Logan's face went white. "I don't—I've never held a baby before."

Rob pulled out his arm. "It's a football, that's it." He set Carter into Logan's cradle, and Logan's eyes went wide.

"He feels like air."

Shar laughed. "Not after four hours."

Logan looked up and met her eyes. "You did good."

"So did you."

Rob grunted. "Except that shift in the second. Looked a little sleepy."

Logan smirked. "You say that while I'm holding your son?"

The guys chatted for a few minutes. Reminiscing, hockey talk. Another moment that felt like a cozy blanket.

I was talking with Maddie when Logan appeared next to me. "Good day?"

I paused mid-sentence and turned. "I've had better."

"Obviously." Logan could barely contain his glee. "Did they do everything? Breakfast, lunch, and—"

"They did more than everything, and I can't believe you put them up to that." I was half aware of the eyes on me, but I couldn't stop smiling. "That was probably the nicest thing anyone's done for me."

"Yeah?" He glanced up to see if anyone heard it, brushing off his shoulder.

"Okay stop, forget I said anything." I pretended to push him, but he caught my arm. My whole body went still.

"You had a good time?"

I nodded, blood rushing in my ears. "The best."

He soaked that in, then dropped my wrist. "Okay. Good."

"Thank you."

"You're welcome."

The air between us thickened, the noise from the conversation around us blending into a low hum.

"Yo, Kemp!" someone shouted, jarring me out of the moment.

Logan turned and held up a finger, then looked back at me. "You want to come out?"

A rope seemed to yank at my middle. *Yes. I'd love to.* "No, I have to pack. I'm heading home for the weekend. Helping with Christmas prep."

Logan's face fell. "Oh. I didn't realize that was tomorrow."

I nodded. "I'll be back Sunday night."

"Got it. Okay, well I'll talk to you then."

"Yep."

He moved to give me hug at the same time I did, but with our height difference and my choice of angle, he ended up giving me a shoulder to the face.

"Geez, Crys—"

"I'm fine. I—"

Logan scooped me against his chest, wrapping his arms around me and holding tight. "Sorry."

For a moment, I couldn't breathe. I was surrounded by warmth and clean soap and strong arms. A sound I'd never made before slipped past my lips, and I snapped my mouth closed. When Logan released me and stepped back, his pupils were blown wide. His lips parted, a flush crawling up his neck.

I blinked and cleared my throat. "Okay. See you soon."

He nodded, a muscle in his jaw jumping. "Mmhmm."

"Have a good night."

Logan drew a quick breath, then turned and stalked back to join his teammates.

Maddie's eyes were on me from across the tunnel, and I knew I was screwed before she even started to mouth, *"That didn't look fake!"*

CHAPTER
Nineteen

I SPENT the weekend at my parents' house, and by hour three I remembered exactly why I both loved it and needed long breaks between weekends home.

The MacMillan household didn't have an "off" switch. The thermostat was permanently two degrees too warm, the TV was always on, even if no one was watching it, and someone was always cooking something with every pan we owned.

My mom threw open the door before I even killed the engine on Rob's truck. "There she is!" She gave me a hug then pushed back to inspect me. "You look thin."

"I'm exactly the same as I was last time you saw me."

She shook her head, then dragged me inside with one arm while simultaneously yelling, "Doug! She's here!"

The kitchen was already a battlefield. Pans everywhere, two cutting boards in active use, my mom's holiday season apron dusted with flour. My dad sat at the table reading a newspaper. Hence the discovery of my relationship with Logan.

He stood when he saw me. "Hey, kiddo." Then, without missing a beat, "We need to discuss this Logan fella."

"Oh my gosh," I groaned. "Dad—"

Thankfully, Mom deposited a plate of food in front of me,

and even though I wasn't especially hungry, I dug in to avoid that conversation.

Lisa showed up twenty minutes later. My older sister, the golden child, still wearing her nursing scrubs.

She dropped her bag on the counter, eyeing my plate before giving me a hug. She stepped back and frowned. "Seriously?"

I whipped my head toward the fridge. There it was. The *Calgary Herald* photo of me and Logan front and center. Paired with my kindergarten handprint turkey Mom always pulled out in the fall.

I covered my face. "Please remove that."

"No," Mom said. "I need it for scrapbooking."

Lisa leaned over the island, chin in her hand. "So. Tell us about hockey boy."

And that pretty much described my first three hours at home. I dodged, deflected, and said things like "We're just working together" through all the cookie baking and Christmas decorating.

By Sunday evening, I was packed and tucked into the freezing truck for the drive back to Calgary. Mom crammed six Tupperwares into my hands. Three soups, two pasta dishes, and something that might have been a taco meat?

"Take the garlic bread too!" Mom shouted from the garage. "You need carbs!"

"I have carbs!" I yelled back.

"Not enough!"

———

I arrived at the gallery warehouse early Monday morning since my regular class was canceled due to my professors unfortunate allergic response to shrimp pasta the night before.

The last of the construction trucks were gone. In their place sat neat stacks of polished floor panels, ladders shoved into corners, and coils of extension cords.

Inside, I stopped dead. The walls gleamed with a fresh coat of crisp white paint, and the track lighting was installed, half the heads already angled toward imaginary canvases.

It didn't look like a warehouse anymore. It looked like a gallery. My gallery.

Norman was already striding across the space with a clipboard, talking to three contractors at once. "Electrical. That corner needs another buff. The southwest panel is warped—replace it. And can someone please fix that outlet?" He pointed, waiting for a response. When he didn't get it, he waved me over like I'd materialized precisely when he needed me. "Crystal. Good. Exhibition sequence today. Start with the emerging artists' alcove. We'll see Alison Kerr at the Palliser. I've got a meeting with her before the reception, and I want a preliminary concept board."

My pulse fluttered. This was a thousand percent better than slashing boxes. "Yes. Absolutely."

"And pull the MacIntyre Foundation file," he added. "Cross-reference this proposal language with our education plan so we don't repeat anything. Or promise anything insane."

Donor proposal language? *He trusted me.* The realization made me heady. I set my stuff down and dove in. I spent the morning ricocheting around the gallery, sketching exhibition flow on tracing paper, labeling plinths with a Sharpie, reviewing lighting angles for both dramatic effect and donor-safe visibility, building the student-engagement binder for the Douglas partnership, and prepping printouts for the meeting with Alison Kerr.

By noon, I felt larger than life, until I realized I'd forgotten the MacIntyre file. Hopefully Norman was still in his office because I didn't have a key.

I approached, noting from down the hall that the door was

propped open, and mentally prepared for a search. Was it a green folder or blue?

I was about to push the door open when I froze.

Norman was in the room, but it wasn't him who stopped my heart in my chest. It was the woman he was kissing.

Alice Kemp.

Logan's mother.

CHAPTER
Twenty

THE PALLISER LOOKED LIKE MONEY. Old money. Leather-bound money. The kind of money that wore cufflinks and got decent-looking hair plugs.

The lobby hummed with soft piano and the dim lighting made everyone look gauzy. Thank the heavens for Shar and her little black dress. If I would've shown up in anything from my wardrobe, I would've looked like someone who wandered in off the street looking for a sunday school class.

Logan's reaction when he picked me up was still playing on repeat in my mind. The slight part of his lips, the quick blinks. I was more prepared since I'd already been blindsided by him in a suit at the breakfast.

Now he walked beside me, suit jacket crisp, hair neat except for one rebellious wave that kept falling onto his forehead. Upstairs, the ballroom doors stood open, spilling out jazz music and chatter. Inside, chandeliers glittered over linen-covered tables and servers carried trays of champagne flutes, offering them to all the guests. Norman glided through the space, greeting everyone.

He found us seconds after we entered. "Crystal. Logan. Excellent. Come, there's someone I want you to meet."

Norman ushered us across the ballroom before I could even get my bearings. A donor I vaguely recognized from the breakfast at Douglas nodded at Logan with thinly veiled awe as we passed.

On a side table near the stage, set discreetly but intentionally beneath spot lighting, hung a large painting. Thick, bold strokes of crimson and navy blues were scraped into geometric motion. At first glance it looked abstract, but then I caught it. The ghost shape of a hockey player mid-stride, the suggestion of a stick, the arc of ice spray.

"Isn't it something?" Norman said, nodding toward the painting.

"It's . . . " I slowed and leaned in to the canvas. "Yes."

Norman had shown me this piece last week. The artist, Olivier Bridet, worked out of Montreal. He used palette knives and varnished pigment. Called it "Kinetic Bodywork" and was doing a series on Canadian sports icons. Trying to capture motion through texture and geometric patterns in space.

I couldn't believe I'd never seen his work before, but he'd apparently refused to consign or display in galleries. The painting in person was mesmerizing, constantly forcing my eyes to sweep in a wide arc instead of stick to the center.

Norman looked pleased. "And this is why you're here. We need to secure Monsieur Bridet for the opening."

What? My stomach twisted like a pair of leggings in the dryer. I thought all of the artists were already on board. And how the hell was I, a college student, supposed to attract an artist at that level?

I reached out for Logan's hand. He turned to me, his eyes widening. *Absolutely necessary.*

The table he led us to was at the front, right next to his board members and the artist's full display. I had no doubt we were about to meet Olivier Bridet himself.

But I couldn't think about that because as we approached, a woman with a blond bob turned to greet us. Alice Kemp.

Her pearl earrings glowed under the chandelier. Her camel coat draped over her chair like a magazine cover. She smiled warmly when she saw us, her eyes flicking to her son with affection.

And then her husband, Logan's dad, turned around. His hand on the small of her back, smiling at Norman like the friend he thought he was.

All I could see, the image flashing in my head, was Alice's mouth on Norman's, her hand on his jaw, the familiarity, the intimacy.

I wanted to throw up.

"Hey." Logan leaned in and kissed her cheek. "I didn't know you'd both be here."

She squeezed his arm, beaming. "We wanted to surprise you."

She was giving a lot of surprises at the moment.

Logan clapped his dad on the back as my insides folded themselves into origami.

"Logan Kemp." A thin man with a tidy beard, wire glasses, and a French accent pushed himself to his feet, interrupting any chance for introductions. He clutched his wine glass like it was a microphone. "I didn't think I'd get to meet you tonight."

Logan dazzled with a smile. "Hey. Nice to meet you, Mr. . . "

"Bridet. Olivier Bridet." He reached out for a handshake. "I've been following you for years. Even before World Juniors."

Logan stiffened almost imperceptibly. I felt it more than saw it. Some tiny hitch in his breath, a fractional tightening of his jaw.

"You were magnifique last season," the man went on. "What was it—eleven points in seven games?"

"Four," Logan corrected gently. "Two goals, two assists."

"Yes! Yes, that's right." The man snapped his fingers, delighted with himself. "And the faceoff percentage. What was it, seventy-six percent?"

"Seventy-three." Logan's smile grew a little tight at the edges.

Since when did he not enjoy bragging about himself? He

squeezed my hand, and I looked over to see Norman, watching the interaction like a hawk.

Then I understood. It wasn't me who was supposed to clinch this contract. It was Logan.

"And the penalty kill," Bridet continued. "Textbook perfect. I remember yelling at my television, 'That's how it's done, that Kemp knows the position!'" He grinned, clearly expecting Logan to laugh.

Logan acquiesced, but Bridet didn't stop there. "It's been a joy watching your career since then," he said, clapping Logan on the shoulder. "Remarkable. Though I'd much prefer you play in Montréal."

"Thank you, that means a lot." Logan turned to take two glasses of champagne from a passing waiter, and Bridet finally turned to me. "You're very lucky. He's a true gem."

I smiled, my mind whirring in the background. What was Logan supposed to do with this? How did Norman expect him to turn this into a gallery sales pitch?

Norman steepled his fingers, gaze sharp. "So. Logan. Tell us how you got to this point. Competition in hockey is cutthroat."

Logan chuckled. "Yeah. You have to be a little obsessive, I think." He glanced up at Alice, and she nodded in agreement.

"From the very beginning, Logan was always driven," she said. "Always aiming higher than the child next to him."

"He didn't settle," Logan's dad added. "If you can give ninety percent, you can give one hundred. Why stop short?"

Logan chuckled, his jaw still tight.

His dad continued, "Principles and work ethic. Excellence is excellence."

Alice picked up the thread without missing a beat. "He delivered, always. Never complacent. Never lazy. Even when he was sick, he'd insist on practice."

"Remember the flu tournament?" His dad chuckled. "He knew he'd set the wrong precedent if he sat out."

Did he know? Or was he told? Logan didn't seem to be

enjoying these anecdotes nearly as much as they were. He wasn't basking in the praise. He was enduring it.

"I know a little of ambition," Bridet murmured, taking another sip of wine.

Logan's hand was ice cold. I saw my opening, and took it. "That kind of work is inspiring. But I think it also comes at a cost."

All the heads turned toward me. I swallowed hard and continued. "Like you said, the competition in hockey is fierce. How many young players have the work ethic but never get the opportunity? It's the same in the art world. That's what's so beautiful about what Norman's doing with this new collective. He's giving a stepping stool to artists who may not have the natural connections or resources that some of us do." I met Logan's gaze. His eyes were fixed on me, and I hoped I wasn't crossing any lines. I ran my thumb over his wrist.

"Like you, Mr. Bridet. You're opening up new possibilities in kinetic art, opening our minds to a new way of presenting movement. But the first time I saw your work was because of Norman. I didn't know it existed." My heart sped up. This was the moment I would likely kill my chances of working in the Calgary art world. "I realize parts of the consignment and display process are problematic for artists, but I hope you'll consider making your work more accessible. Young artists like me need to see what's possible. We need more Logans in the world to inspire us."

I picked up the champagne glass Logan had set in front of me and took a sip. The bubbles popped on my tongue, giving me something else to focus on besides my trembling fingers.

Logan looked at me then, and something flickered behind his eyes. He dropped my hand and slipped his arm around my waist, pulling me close. His warmth enveloped me, and I let out an involuntary sigh of relief.

What was happening between us? Logan wasn't anything like I expected based on Shar's description of their relationship.

He was attentive and kind. That surprise he pulled with the Outlaws? I'd never been treated more like royalty in my life.

But Shar's words clanged in my head like a church bell. *I don't want you to get hurt.*

Bridet tapped his wine glass, his brow furrowed. "I can't say I've ever considered that."

I had to remind myself what our topic of conversation was. *What had I said that he hadn't considered?* Something about making his work more accessible?

A woman who'd been silent until that moment spoke up. "I agree wholeheartedly. There's too much gatekeeping in this industry, and the old guard is dying off." She shrugged when Alice frowned at that comment. "It's true. We need new blood and we're not going to get it if the barriers to entry are too high."

The woman put out a hand toward me, and I shook it. "Alison Kerr. Glenbow Museum."

So, this was who Norman was talking about the other day. I liked her already. "Crystal MacMillan."

Norman's eyes gleamed, turning the attention back to Bridet. "I'd love to discuss options for a feature in December . . ." He closed in, and I sank into Logan.

"Thank you," he murmured when the conversation had thankfully turned away from us.

I played it off, taking another sip of champagne. I'd hoped it would settle my pulse, but it wasn't working. Not when Alice kept laughing at Logan's dad's jokes, all while her gaze kept slipping to Norman.

I had to tell him. I couldn't keep this in my body, and he deserved to know. But how did you drop a bomb like that on someone? Or . . . was it possible he already knew? Alice did spend a lot of time with Norman, and Logan didn't seem especially close with his dad. Was it a secret he was in on?

That thought dropped a pile of rocks into my gut. No. He wouldn't do that to someone, would he? Even if he and his dad had issues, would he keep a secret like that? Knowing how hurtful it was?

"You okay?" Logan asked.

I nodded, pretending to be listening when all I could hear was white noise. I couldn't eat. I still accepted food that was offered and took small bites, then found opportunities to hide the rest in my napkin. When Logan finally took a break to use the washroom, I snatched my chance to escape.

I ducked into the ladies' room, my stomach pitching so hard I thought I might faint onto the marble countertop. I braced my hands on the cool sink, willing my breathing to slow. "Pull it together," I whispered to myself. "You're fine."

But I wasn't fine. And I wasn't going to make it through the rest of the night unless I talked to Logan. I splashed cold water on my wrists, dabbed beneath my eyes, and straightened my dress.

The hallway outside the ballroom was quieter. Soft carpet, dark wood panelling, low lamps. I caught sight of Logan's silhouette exiting the washroom and intercepted him.

"Hey, what—?"

Laughter sounded down the hall, and a group rounded the corner. I didn't want to look like we were hiding or having an intense conversation, so I did the only thing my panicking brain could think of.

I pressed into him, pushing Logan back against the wall and sliding a hand up his chest.

His hands flew to my waist on instinct. "Whoa—okay."

"Shh," I hissed. "I need to talk to you."

His fingers tightened, his confusion melting into performance. He angled his body, dipped his head close to mine, breath warm against my ear. To anyone watching, we looked like two people who couldn't wait to get a hotel room.

Absolutely necessary?

His thumb brushed my hip through the fabric of my dress, and my pulse bucked.

"What's going on?" he murmured.

"I'm going to tell you something. I was hoping to wait until later, but I don't think I can."

His throat caught. "Okay."

I swallowed hard, fingers curling against his lapel. "And if you're already aware, then . . . I don't know. You better have a good explanation."

His breathing quickened. "Not loving that, but got it."

"I saw something," I whispered. "At the gallery. With your mom and Norman."

His hand froze. His body went rigid.

I kept my face turned slightly toward his neck, my lips millimetres from his skin.

"They were kissing, Logan."

No breath. No sound. No movement. After ten seconds, I worried his heart had handed in its two weeks' notice.

"You're sure?" His voice was clipped.

"Positive. I didn't mean to spy," I explained in a rush. "The door was cracked. I was returning to the office to grab a file. And . . . did you know?"

It was like someone flipped a switch. "No." His hands slid off my waist. I stepped back, searching his face. His eyes were blank, like a shutter had been slammed down. "Thanks for telling me."

"Logan—"

"We should go back in."

I reached for his arm, but he moved away from me.

"No," he said. Not sharp. Not angry. Just final. "Later." And then he turned and strode back into the ballroom.

I took a moment, feeling somehow worse than when I'd entered the washroom. By the time I arrived at the table, Logan had already reclaimed his seat. His hands were folded, his face pleasant.

Norman lifted his champagne glass. "I'm glad you're back. I wanted to make sure you were here for this announcement."

I didn't think I could take much more excitement for one night.

Norman waited for the full attention of the table. "We'll be hosting a private retreat at Banff Springs November 21-23."

November 21-23. Was that on our contract? I thought back to the document, to the dates Norman had scribbled in. *November 21. TBD.* This was a pretty damn big TBD.

"Key partners only," he continued. "Creative strategy, board introductions, a preview of the gallery program." He looked at Logan, then at me. "We'll be conducting community giving opportunities in conjunction with the Blizzard and cultural education sponsored by Douglas. I can't wait for you both to participate."

IT WAS as if someone pulled the plug on Logan Kemp. I didn't hear from him all week. My calls went to his voicemail, and I did leave a few messages. He was away at a game for at least part of the time, but that hadn't stopped him from calling the last time.

I doubted he was angry with me, but it was still heavy. I couldn't imagine what he was going through or what kind of fallout there was after the Palliser. I wanted to help.

Since I couldn't, I dug into work. The gallery was in that strange in-between stage now. No longer a construction zone, but not yet an actualized space. The walls were finished, the floors sealed, the track lights installed. The air smelled like fresh paint instead of wet concrete.

Norman had me doing tasks I enjoyed, and it was easier to separate him from what I'd seen when we were focused on the opening.

We spent one morning crawling through the floor plan with tracing paper overlays, sketching how the emerging-artist alcove would flow into the main exhibition space. Another afternoon we stood under the lights, testing brightness and warmth against a generic canvas. I started a spreadsheet, my new religion, tracking works, sizes, mediums, proposed placements, and "conversation partners" (Norman's term) across the room.

On Thursday he set a stack of folders on the edge of his desk and tapped it. "Student applications. I'd like your take before I make final selections. Two or three pieces for the opening."

"What are you looking for?"

"Perspective. You have yours. I'd like to hear it."

I dragged the stack over and started working through it, one by one. Photos of sculptural installations made from recycled material. Etchings of suburban houses with ominous shadows. A series of small canvases exploring light through lace curtains.

One piece stopped me cold.

It was a triptych of monoprints. A repeated image of a figure mid-stride, torso twisting, limbs blurring, the ink pushed and pulled across the plate so the body almost dissolved into motion. Each print was slightly different, like someone had captured three frames of a film and smeared them before they set.

There were no cover sheets, so I had no idea who had done it, but I instantly set it in my "yes" pile. By the time I finished the stack, I had three firm picks and two "maybe if we have more space" pieces. I brought them over to Norman, my notes scribbled in the margins.

I hoped we'd have a conversation about it, but his attention stalled when his office door swung open.

"Well, good afternoon you two." Logan's mom swept in, her light, floral perfume invading the room.

She greeted me with a hug, then embraced Norman.

My smile froze in place. If she knew I knew, she didn't show it. If Logan had confronted her, there was no sign.

Which meant he likely hadn't.

I didn't know what to think about that. There were a thousand reasons why he may have kept that information to himself, but I had none of them since he'd gone radio silent.

I missed the Blizzard game that night. I said it was because I had packing to do, but really, I couldn't imagine watching Logan on the ice when I knew what was going on in the background.

When I woke up the next morning to the little red light on my answering machine and heard Logan's voice, I nearly choked on my Shreddies.

"Hey, Crystal." *Not Crys.* "Just confirming tomorrow—pick you up at eight? I'm making up a training session in the morning, so it might be closer to eight-fifteen. See you then."

Normal.

Like nothing had happened at all.

CHAPTER
Twenty~Two

I TRIED to broach real topics on our drive, but Logan was a steel lock box. He smoothly transitioned away from talk about family or friends and instead asked about my classes, then happily rehashed the game from the night before after I made my excuses for missing it.

The trip went by in a blink, and I couldn't hide my pure delight when we pulled up to the Banff Springs. I'd seen it before, but not since I was a kid. Up close, it was a fairytale castle with stone turrets, sloping roofs, and warm, glowing windows. The mountains rose behind it like they were posing for a photograph.

Logan pulled into the circular drive and waited in the valet line. I'd never done valet parking in my life.

"Ready?" he asked, handing one of the staff his keys.

I nodded. He insisted on unloading the bags, and we headed inside the lobby.

The stone arches and plush carpets took my breath away. A fireplace crackled in one corner. Someone's child climbed a leather chair and got gently peeled off by a woman who, by how young she looked, had to be the nanny.

Norman had arranged our reservation and left our names

with the front desk staff. The attendant typed a few things into the computer and handed over two keycards in a branded cardboard sleeve.

"Standard king room. Third floor. Mountain view."

My eyes widened. Umm, only one room? I was about to protest, when Logan took the keys. "Great. Thanks."

We stepped into the elevator. The doors slid shut, and I stared at the buttons.

"All good?" Logan cocked his head to the side.

"Uh, no. Not all good. I wasn't planning to—I thought we'd both have our own room."

He raised an eyebrow. "Why?"

I started at least three responses in my head, but didn't answer. *Why had I thought that?* Norman believed we were together. I was suddenly regretting not going the Amish route with my refusal to do photographs.

"Yeah. I don't know. I didn't think it through, I guess."

The elevator dinged.

"It's a sleepover. It'll be fun."

Everything out of Logan's mouth was something he would've said before the Palliser. Before I told him about Alice and Norman. But now, his words didn't hold the same warmth. They were empty shells, sketched outlines, and I was desperate to reel in a sliver of that old connection.

"My parents didn't let me have sleepovers," I murmured.

Logan laughed as we stepped out into a gorgeous carpeted hall. Our room was at the end. He swiped the keycard and pushed the door open with his shoulder.

I stepped in behind him, my heart fluttering like a butterfly trapped in a jar. One king bed. Headboard. Fancy pillows. One kitchenette, an armchair. One small table. One bathroom door to the right.

"You're very calm about this," I said, as Logan set our bags down.

He shrugged, wandered over to the window, and pushed the

curtain aside. "Grew up sharing rooms on the road. Bus bunks, motel double beds, couches. Not that different."

I tried not to take offense to him comparing me to his hockey boys, but the snark still snuck into my voice. "You're right. This isn't different at all."

He gave me a look. "That's not what I meant."

"Well, it's what you said." I couldn't help getting a little snippy. Why couldn't we just talk about what happened? Get back to where we were before?

Logan walked into the room, leaning a shoulder against the window frame. The mountain view behind him was painting worthy. Peaks, trees, little rivers of light from the town below. His silhouette didn't hurt the view one bit.

"Relax, MacMillan. We'll figure it out. You get the bed. I'll take the chair. Or the floor. I've slept on worse."

"You are not sleeping on the floor of the Banff Springs."

He turned, a smirk on his lips. "We could have a pillow fight if that would make you feel better. That's what you and your roommates do, right?"

I laughed. "Oh, every night. In only our panties."

"Perfect." Logan gave a wolfish smile, and my throat thickened.

"You're gross, Kemp."

"I'm not the one who brought up panties."

I cringed. Yeah, that was my bad. I glanced at the clock on the microwave. "Okay, we'll resume negotiations later. We're going to be late."

We took turns in the bathroom to change, and I couldn't help but notice there was a double shower head and a seat in the shower. I tried to keep my imagination at bay as I put on tight black slacks and a blouse I'd borrowed from Jenna. Logan changed into khakis and a Polo shirt, and I wondered if he'd made the same observations I had.

When we joined the others, Logan looked like he belonged there. I felt like I was playing dress up.

We made it through our lunch and the educational sessions that afternoon. Well, I did that portion. Logan took a nap in the hotel room.

The evening mixer was in one of the lower ballrooms. Strings of white lights draped from the beams, making the atmosphere dreamy. Just like the Palliser, servers flitted around with trays of wine and tiny appetizers.

Norman was already in full schmooze mode, flanked by board members, a couple of politicians, and a handful of people I recognized from earlier grant paperwork. I could pick out the MacIntyre Foundation guy by his eyebrows alone.

Logan and I were separated almost instantly. Norman wanted me to talk with one of the politicians, a woman from the province's Arts Secretariat, and Logan was pulled away by his Blizzard administration team. Two other players were there, not Rourke or Haines, but I didn't get a chance to meet them.

I tried to snag him when we moved toward dinner, but he was nowhere to be found. Thankfully, I ended up at a table with Alison Kerr.

We made small talk through the salad course, but when the main dishes were brought out, it finally got interesting. We dove into a philosophical discussion about experimental art, and though I didn't have much to add, I had plenty of questions.

I absorbed every provocative opinion she dished out and scrambled to keep up, occasionally saying something that made her eyes light up.

I didn't realize I'd downed two full glasses of red wine until Logan showed up, and I couldn't remember why it'd been so awkward before.

"Hey!" I pushed my chair back and stood, wrapping my arms around his neck.

He chuckled. "Seems you've been having fun."

"You have to meet Allison," I said, motioning for him to join us. The man seated there earlier had left before dessert.

We both chatted for the last few minutes, said our goodbyes, and thanked Norman for the meal. Allison gave me her card, and I was on cloud nine by the time Logan and I made it back to the room. The buzz from the wine was dissipating, but I was still flying high on the conversation and connections.

How was this my life? How had I gone from anxious art student with zero prospects for the spring to rubbing shoulders with the most powerful decision makers in the province?

Logan Kemp was how.

I closed the door behind us with a soft click. "You're incredible, you know that?"

Logan's mouth quirked. "Tell me more."

I laughed. "I'm serious. None of this would've happened if you hadn't introduced me to Norman Marcus."

There was a small flash of something in Logan's face, and it sobered me. *Right.* He probably didn't want to hear anything about Norman at the moment.

I pulled a glass from the cupboard in the galley kitchen and gulped down some water. "Do you mind if I shower first?"

Logan shook his head. "No problem." He dropped onto the couch, picking up the TV remote. "The Oilers are playing tonight."

My eyes lit up. I'd never watched a game with Logan. He'd always been on the ice. "Okay. I'll hurry."

Logan was right. I needed to stop stressing about this whole room situation. We'd make it work just like we made everything else work in this crazy relationship scenario.

Maybe I needed to stop stressing about everything. People needed time to process new information, and the story I'd told him was a straight up bomb to the life he knew. I should cut him some slack.

I rushed into the bathroom and pushed my hair to the side to unzip my blouse, and frowned. The zipper wouldn't budge.

I twisted in the mirror, perching on the counter to try and see what the problem was, but I couldn't get a good angle. I tried pulling the blouse off without unzipping, but there was no way that was happening. Finally I gave up and walked back out to the living room.

The game was on, but Logan wasn't sitting on the couch. My stomach dropped to my knees when I found him shirtless, his bag open on the bed.

The muscles in his back flexed, moving under his skin like ripples as he reached for a new shirt. His pants were undone, slipping off his hip on the right side, showing the line of his boxer briefs.

My mouth went dry, and I forced my eyes down to the carpet. "Um, can you help me?" I spun as fast as humanly possible and pointed to the back of my blouse. "I can't get this zipper undone."

"Oh, yeah." He walked over too fast to have remedied his state of undress. *Had he even buttoned up his pants?*

I shivered as his fingers brushed my neck.

"Sorry. Cold hands."

I coughed. "No, it's fine."

He brushed my hair further to the side, leaving a trail of heat along my skin. "I think the fabric is stuck."

"Yeah, it wouldn't move for me."

He fiddled with the mechanism. "I don't want to rip it."

"Well, I have to take it off, so if it rips, I'll get Jenna a new one."

"This is Jenna's?" He tugged on the fabric, and I nodded. "It looks good on you."

My stomach swooped. "Thanks."

Logan let out a grunt. "My fingers are too fat." He did have large hands. "I'm just going to—"

I gasped as his breath hit the back of my neck.

"—use my teeth."

Logan's lips tickled my skin as he caught the fabric and tugged. "Got it," he murmured, his voice rumbling through me. His hands landed back on my shoulders, dragging the zipper down with deliberate care. The little metal teeth made a soft *tick-*

tick-tick sound as they parted. Cool air hit my skin as his fingertips brushed my spine.

When had I closed my eyes?

"What's this from?" Logan parted the fabric, touching the middle of my back.

I swallowed, my throat thick. "Waterslide. I scraped the skin there, and the pigment never came back."

"Hmm." His hand still hovered, and gooseflesh pricked my skin.

I could have stepped away. Probably should have, but I didn't. I stood there, waiting.

Logan's hand trailed back up, tracing the knuckles of my spine, then pausing at the edge of the fabric. He brushed it over the edge of my shoulder, fingering the strap of my bra.

I tilted my head, exposing my neck, remembering what it felt like when his lips hovered there in the hall of the Palliser.

I sucked in a breath as he moved in closer. His left hand threaded through my hair, tilting my head further, and as he curled over me, his lips finally meeting the tender skin stretched open for him, heat crackled through my veins.

My hand shot up, cupping his jaw, pulling him closer.

This. I wanted this. Something. Anything. Maybe we couldn't get there in words at the moment, but in just a few short weeks, this connection we shared had grown to eclipse every other relationship in my life.

That realization sent a jolt down my spine. Did Logan feel the same way? He always seemed excited to talk, and he'd gone out of his way to help me, multiple times. Was that his way of telling me his feelings were changing, too? Was that why he was kissing me now?

Logan spun me to face him, twisting me in his arms. His breath was minty, his scruff rough against my cheek.

Was I going to stop this? I considered it. But then Logan's mouth met mine, and as my hands splayed against his chest, I realized there was no way in hell they'd be willing to let go.

CHAPTER
Twenty~Three

LOGAN'S SKIN was like crushed velvet, and I was instantly drunk on the way he enveloped me. His strength was raw, his size all-consuming compared to mine. Every part of me felt dainty, more fragile.

He deepened the kiss, one hand sliding around my waist and pulling me flush against him, the other still cradling the back of my neck. The blouse slipped lower, baring both my shoulders, slipping to my elbows.

My hands found his waist, and the feel of his abs tensing against my thumbs was like lighter fluid over smouldering coals. I ignited, every connection point between us becoming a live wire.

His tongue brushed my lower lip, and I opened for him, our mouths slowing to explore new territory. He was gentle, tentative. Toying with me until my fingertips dug into his back.

I didn't remember moving, but the wall materialized behind me, and Logan pressed me against it. His hand slid from my hair and cupped my bra, his fingers teasing the edges of the fabric.

The tremor in his exhale and the slight shiver in his fingers forced my blood south. When he hitched me up, lifting me off the floor so we were the same height, I wrapped my legs around his waist and—

The phone trilled, and I gasped, nearly knocking my head into Logan's. Both of us froze, panting. Another ring.

I dropped my legs, and Logan let me slide back to the floor, but didn't release me. My hands were still looped around his neck, and his head curled over, resting against the wall.

Who was calling our hotel room at nine o'clock at night?

Logan pushed off the wall and stalked to the nightstand, picking up the handset. "Hello?" His voice was rough, his pants still hanging halfway off his hips. I pulled the blouse back up, crossing my arms so it would stay put.

"Mmhmm. No, I know." Logan's entire body tensed, the muscles in his back pulling together. I was dying to know who was on the other end of the line. "It was good. Yep. I think he was happy with it." Another long pause. "I'll pass it along. Okay. Goodnight, Mom."

The heat that, up until that second, had been coursing through me, fizzled like Logan had doused me with a bucket of ice-cold water.

He hung up the phone, drew a deep breath, then turned to face me. His eyes were dark, almost haunted in the light of the lamp.

"Sorry," Logan murmured, his voice rough.

"Mmm." I couldn't put together an actual sentence.

Logan scrubbed a hand over his jaw, and his furrowed brow told me whatever moment we just had was over. My shoulders sagged a little.

"She wanted me to give a message to Norman," he continued.

I didn't know what to say to that, so I stood there, letting the elephant take up all the space in the room. Multiple elephants, really.

Two seconds ago, I'd been kissing Logan Kemp. *Shar's ex.* While my friends knew I was spending time with him—they'd more than encouraged it—what would they say to this? Would they be as supportive if they knew it wasn't exactly an accident? That I'd thought about this more times than I could count? That I looked forward to calling him after dinner? That not talking with him over the last week had felt like a piece of myself had gone missing?

But the interruption also reminded me why I'd been so eager to be close to him. Because there was a large, Norman-shaped wedge between us. I needed to yank it out.

"Have you talked to your mom about Norman?" I asked.

He shook his head. "There's nothing to talk about."

My lips pursed. "I think there's one pretty big thing to—"

"How will that help anything?" He dropped to the bed, resting his arms on his knees. "Things are fine. My parents seem as happy as ever—"

"But they're obviously not happy." What was Logan even saying? If things were fine, his mom wouldn't be shacking up with an art icon.

Logan blew out a breath. "I don't know. I'm not going to make a big deal out of it."

My heart started to race. "You're not the one who made a big deal out of anything. That was your mom, Logan. She's the one who decided to have an affair. Don't you think your dad deserves to know? Don't you deserve to hear the truth from her?"

He lowered his head, dragging his fingers through his hair. "And then what? My parents get divorced? They hate each other? No, if they're fine like this then—"

"They're not *fine*," I snapped, my chest so tight, I thought it might crack at the seams. How was he being so obtuse? There were things you let go in a relationship and things you didn't. I needed to make that more obvious.

"Is this how you would've dealt with things with Shar? If she'd never seen that picture in the paper, would you have just pretended it never happened? Since things were *fine?* Easier not to rock the boat?"

Logan met my eyes, his jaw tight. "No."

"You sure about that?" I honestly wondered. The way he was treating this, so flippant. It set off alarm bells in my head.

He sniffed. "No, I wouldn't have. Things weren't fine between us. I already told you that."

"But Shar was the one who brought it up."

"Does it matter?"

"Yes, it matters! If you want a relationship with someone, you have to be willing to talk about the things that are hard."

Logan let out a sardonic laugh. "If you want a relationship with someone, you tow the line. You do what they want, and when you find out that it wasn't good enough, you give them something else to hopefully make it okay again, and when that's not good enough, you get over it and move on. End of story."

I pursed my lips, my heart sinking like a rock. Was he mad, or was that his honest-to-goodness version of the truth? Was his relationship with his parents his model for life? "Is that what you think a relationship is?"

A muscle popped in his jaw. "At least when I disappoint my parents, they don't walk out with my best friend."

Something inside of me shattered like I'd accidentally stepped on a Christmas ornament. I'd seen enough in the few interactions between Logan and his parents to have a feel for their dynamic.

My parents didn't own a bunch of houses in the city or have impressive political connections, but they'd never once made me feel like I wasn't good enough or that I had to accomplish something to earn their love and approval.

I took a step closer, leaving the safety of the wall. "Logan—"

"I'm fine, Crys. I was just making a point."

I shook my head, taking another step. "You don't need to be fine, though. That's *my* point. It's okay to be pissed about how everything went down in the spring. And it's okay to feel hurt and angry about—"

"I'm not pissed! I was the problem in that relationship, I get it. I was selfish, and I honestly don't know why Shar stayed so long in the first place. It's not like I was offering her anything to be excited about."

"But she didn't talk to you either. She was doing exactly what you're doing now with your mom. She wanted to keep the peace, so she didn't speak up, and that never works. Not if you want something real."

"Why do you care?" Logan wet his lips, his body restless. "It's not like you're dating me."

His words sliced through me. Well, my words actually. I'd said that to him at the beginning of all this, and technically, it was still true.

Logan stood and walked back to his suitcase. "Maybe I'm not meant for something real. Maybe fake is the best it gets."

That felt personal. "Hm. Nice."

"No, I'm serious. What's so bad about fake? We get to hang out together, talk. I'm having fun, aren't you?"

Something about his tone set my teeth on edge. "Pretty sure you could have fake whenever you wanted, Logan. That's kind of what started this whole thing."

"No, I don't mean sex. Though if a fake relationship had more benefits—" He froze, turning to me with a shirt in his hands, and my heart stalled at the expression on his face. "Wait. What if it did?"

I tucked the loose edge of the blouse under my bra strap. "What if—what?"

"Our fake relationship. What if it had benefits?"

"That is a terrible idea," I blurted. The words were mostly for myself because I was now imagining picking up where we left off before the phone call.

A cocky grin spread across his face. "I don't know, is it?"

His chest and abs were messing with my logic.

"Think about it," he continued. "We're spending time together anyway. You even said that pretending to be my girl-friend meant you couldn't have sex for a month, so what if you could have lots of sex for the month?"

I laughed out loud. "That's your pitch? You tell me that it's not about sex, but then suggest this?" Goosebumps rose on my skin. With my shirt undone and Logan no longer warming me, I was getting chilled.

Logan opened his mouth, then closed it again, the smile falling from his eyes. "It wouldn't just be about that."

"Oh, yeah? What would it be about, then?"

Logan searched my face, the wheels turning in his head. Finally, he said, "I need your help with something."

I gave him a look. "Does the first word start with a 'B' and the second a 'J?'"

He smirked. "No, but that's not off the table."

I feigned relief. "Well, thank goodness for that."

Logan's throat bobbed. "I was thinking more . . . something for you."

Tingles shot down my legs. What was happening right now? If someone had burst in and told me Logan was reading from a rom-com script, I would've believed them. Two people, trapped in a fake relationship and a castle hotel room . . .

The script practically wrote itself.

"Wait, I'm not following. Pleasuring me is what *you* need help with?"

He huffed out a breath, eyes darting to me and then away again. *Was Logan Kemp nervous?* "I've never had to work hard for sex. That's not bragging, it's just true. It was always easy to get what I wanted." He shifted on his feet. "I took advantage of that. Got what I wanted. Didn't think that much about whether I was actually . . . giving them anything in return.

"After Shar, I started thinking about it differently. About what I did. What I didn't do. What I never even thought about asking." He looked up again, and that time, his eyes were liquid.

The fire I thought the phone call had extinguished? It was back to a full blaze. Logan twisted the shirt in his hands. "You could teach me."

The word "teach" should not have done to my nervous system what it did. No thoughts or words would compute. *Was he serious?* He seemed pretty damn serious. The idea of Logan touching me, experimenting with me, asking me what I wanted . . .

"Look," he said. "We're both adults. We both know this is temporary. There's an endpoint. Gallery opens, our relationship ends, we go back to being friends. It doesn't have to be more than that."

There was that tone again. The shutter behind his eyes. Those warning sirens went off like fireworks on Canada Day.

While he was talking about this being purely educational, my subconscious knew that what I'd felt pressed against the wall was more than interesting information. 'Friends' was quickly becoming the second-best, and far inferior, option in my version of this scenario.

It didn't matter that Logan had opened the door wide on his relationship dysfunction. That he just said our relationship had an endpoint, dashing any hopes I'd fostered that he might be questioning this like I was.

Just like I should have walked back to the bathroom after the zipper was undone, I should've run for the shower now. This was not going to end well. I was already getting attached, I could feel it, and sex? That was not going to make things any simpler.

I swallowed the lump in my throat. "Just to be clear. You're suggesting that I . . . be your sex tutor."

His neck flushed. "If it sounds fun to you. Yeah."

If it sounded fun? Hell yes, it sounded fun. Carte blanche to do whatever I wanted for the next three weeks? Logan dedicating himself to *my* pleasure until we broke up? I couldn't think of anything more fun, which made me desperate for something to ground me.

I couldn't blame Shar, and I definitely couldn't play my whole hand and admit I was worried about getting attached. So, I laid down the only other card I had. "I doubt your parents would approve."

It was supposed to be funny, or at least not offensive, but Logan's expression darkened. "I don't give a rat's ass what they approve of or don't."

Well. That was fair. But it didn't alleviate my stress reaction. "You know every woman's body is different. What I like might not be—"

"No, I know." He rubbed a hand over his neck. "If you don't want—"

"I didn't say that. I'm just—" I exhaled in a rush. "What if I'm not very helpful?" I hoped he'd read between the lines. I'd only ever been with two people, and while it wasn't terrible, it definitely wasn't something to write Cosmopolitan about.

Logan didn't hesitate. "I've told you things I've never told anyone, and I think you feel comfortable being honest with me." He waited for me to nod. "Right. So, I don't think that's possible."

My heart lurched. If he was trying to flatter me, it was working. I searched for any other rebuttal, but came up empty. Unless I wanted to hammer another wedge between us, there was only one thing left to do.

"Okay," I squeaked.

Logan's pupils dilated. He glanced at the bed, then at my half-removed blouse. "Shower?"

Twenty~Four

I PRESSED myself against the closed bathroom door, my heart racing. It turned out Logan had, in fact, noticed the double shower head when he was changing. I wondered if he'd been thinking about it since lunch, but didn't have the guts to ask. Had he planned this? Did he think when he'd told me not to worry about the bed situation, that this was a possibility?

He kicked his pants to the side and turned to face me in only his boxer briefs, which meant I had a full view of his front and back, courtesy of the wall-length mirror.

My pulse swooped.

Logan leaned on the counter. "We don't have to do this. It's never too late to call it off."

I wet my lips, my eyes travelling down his torso. "He says, standing in front of me, nearly naked."

Logan raised an eyebrow. "Is that a factor in your decision-making?"

"No." I lied, forcing my gaze back to his.

"It *is* educational. You can do your own research too, if you want."

I bit my lip. "Just—turn around."

He grinned. "Starting already?"

"No, I just don't want you watching—"

"Hell, no!" Logan laughed. "If we're doing this, you don't get to tell me not to watch."

I thought about pushing the issue, but what was the point? If, in fact, I was going through with this, we were going to be naked in the shower in about five seconds.

Despite my stomach lurching, I let go of the blouse and let it fall to my hips, then quickly unbuttoned my black slacks and slid them off with the shirt in tow. I dropped them onto Logan's pants and stood there in my underwear, hyper-aware of every inch of exposed skin. Of the way the bathroom light hit my curves and lack thereof, the soft not-quite-flatness of my stomach.

"Can I—" Logan's voice caught. He lifted a hand, motioning to my bra. I nodded and turned, giving him access to the clasp.

Air hissed through my teeth as his fingers brushed my skin.

"Do most bras have two clasps or three?"

I blinked, trying to focus. "Depends. Most of mine have two, but I do have a couple that are three. The cute ones only have two."

He made a sound, fiddling with the band. The tension released. Just like before, I waited. Logan slipped the straps off my shoulders, and I straightened my arms, letting it fall to the floor.

"Do you like that?" he asked.

"What?"

"Me taking it off?"

I nodded. "Yes."

He stepped back, and I counted to three, gathering the courage to turn. When I did, his eyes swept over me. Slow, but not leering, no smirk on his lips.

"You're beautiful," he said simply.

My insides liquified. "That's . . . a smart thing to say. Women like that."

Logan's brow twitched. He hesitated a moment, then

nodded. "Got it." He turned and pushed the shower door to the side, flipping on the water to hot, then walked to the other side to turn on the second head.

He spun back and looped his thumbs in his underwear.

"Wait." My face turned crimson in the mirror. "I—it's fine, you can—I just thought—"

"No, you can take them off." He dropped his arms.

While I couldn't speak for all women, I had a hard time believing a single one of them wouldn't find this a huge turn-on. In the two more serious relationships I'd had, I'd never felt like I was going to pass out in their presence.

Was it Logan's questions? His desire to learn? The fact that we'd talked for weeks or that he'd picked me up when my car stalled? That we'd gotten interrupted during our makeout session, and I didn't get what I wanted?

Logan wanted to know what I liked, but I was probably the more curious of the two of us. Had I ever asked myself what I liked—what I wanted—and explored the answers?

I closed the gap between us and reached for his boxers, dragging them lower over his hips. It took a second to figure out where they were stuck—Logan laughed at that—but eventually, I succeeded.

When I tried to step back, he caught my waist and returned the favour. I about died of embarrassment as he pulled my underwear over my knees, his face inches from me.

We stood in front of each other, assessing. Curiosity didn't begin to cover what I felt in that moment. In the past, I'd always been worried about doing the right thing, but Logan had given me permission to wonder. I wanted to touch every part of him. Explore and figure out how everything worked.

"Your body is . . . " I shook my head. I didn't have the right word for it. It wasn't just that I was turned on by him. It was art.

Logan's eyes flared, and I realized I'd said the words out loud. It was true. I wished I had a sketchbook, something to capture the perfect lines of his torso, the shading under his pecs, the gentle curve of his shoulders juxtaposed with the rough line of his jaw.

His breathing quickened. "Men like that."

For a moment, I regretted everything. I should've said something, been honest with him about how I wasn't totally sure this was all fake for me anymore. I didn't want to say that to other men. I wanted to say it to him.

Logan opened the shower door, releasing a cloud of steam that billowed around us. He stepped in first, moving so I could follow.

The heat soaked into my skin, sending shivers down my spine. I pulled the pins from my hair and set them in the soap dish, then tilted my head into the stream. When I wiped the water from my face, I found Logan in front of me, holding the tiny bottle of hotel body wash.

"Turn around?" he murmured.

My heart jolted. What was it about having him behind me that sent my head into a tailspin?

Logan moved in close, building gravity that my body fell toward before I could stop it. The click of the cap. The hiss of the water. It all sounded in slow motion.

He didn't move for a moment. I could *feel* his gaze on me, like a fingertip tracing just above the surface, not quite touching. Heat coiled low in my stomach. Then his hand landed on my back, and he smoothed the soap between my shoulder blades.

"How's this?" he asked quietly.

Good? Perfect? "Nice," I managed, though it came out half breathless. His hand slid down the curve of my spine, and my eyes fluttered closed.

"Pressure okay?" he asked.

I grinned. "You're not going to break me."

His hands glided over my body, smooth and soft. "Tell me if you want me to stop."

I didn't ever want him to stop. This was the most soothing,

erotic thing anyone had ever done for me. I struggled to fill my lungs.

When Logan finished, he spun me around to rinse the soap from my back. He blinked, heavy lidded, water from his shower head flicking off his shoulders and landing on my cheeks.

"Can I?" I held my hand out for the bottle, but Logan hesitated. "No? I didn't—"

"I want you to. But . . ." Logan struggled to find the words.

"But?"

"I'm really far gone."

My brow pinched. "What—?" He pointed down, and my eyes dropped. *Oh.*

"This is why I never ask women what they want. It's not because I don't want to know, it's because I'm worried you'll—they'll—be disappointed when I try to do it and can't last."

I worked to engage my rational brain. "So what if you can't?"

Logan huffed a laugh. "Um, then it's kind of over."

"No, it's not." I pushed my hair from my face. "Did you ever think that you not lasting would actually be something I liked?"

He stared at me blankly. "I don't even know what to say to that."

"You being so turned on, you can't touch me and not respond? That's like . . . I don't even know. Like crack for my brain."

He laughed out loud. "It's embarrassing."

"Why? Because you're supposed to be some sex God? Honestly, if a guy lasted too long, I'd wonder if there was something wrong with me."

His expression sobered. "You're serious."

"Yeah. I'm serious."

"So, you wouldn't be disappointed?"

I shook my head. "Only if he rolled over and stopped there."

"But if he didn't . . ."

I chewed on my lower lip, debating how honest I was feeling. "Then I'd be a little worried about taking too long myself."

He looked away, his brow furrowing. "Does it take long?"

My eyes widened, and I quickly schooled my expression. "You don't know?"

He cleared his throat. "I'm just . . . I don't know if I've ever done it right."

I took the bottle from his hands. "Yeah. It can take a long time. Especially when you haven't been together before."

"Do you ever pretend?"

I couldn't help but laugh. "Ever? Try every single time."

He blinked. "You're joking."

I wished I was. "Not joking."

He stepped closer, planting his hands on my hips. "No." My breath caught. He shook his head, water droplets from his hair landing on my skin. "Don't ever pretend with me, okay?"

"But what if I can't—"

"No, we'll figure it out. How can I get better if I don't know what I'm doing wrong?"

I thought of Bridet, the hockey artist at the dinner table. *I'd honestly never thought about it that way before.* "But, Logan, when I say a *long* time—"

"I don't give a shit. Don't pretend. Worst case scenario, we just get to spend more time doing something that's pretty great."

I looked up at him, hot water streaming down my back. Was this a promise I could keep? I decided it was at least one worth trying for. "Okay."

He nodded in approval. "Good." Logan's hands slid from my hips, and he turned.

My pulse skipped as I poured the body wash into my hands and lathered it. He stood still, water slicking down his shoulders, one arm out, pressed against the tile.

My palms slid over the broad muscles of his upper back, and he flinched. "Is that okay?"

He chuckled, his hand reaching back to pull me closer. "You might not be breakable, Crys, but I think I am."

I pressed closer, dropping my head and pressing my cheek against his skin. His hand squeezed on my thigh, warm water coursing from his body to mine.

Logan growled low in his throat, his hand circling my wrist as he turned to face me. "You'll have to do that later." He dropped his head, kissing me, rough and desperate.

I felt for the soap dish and set the bottle there with my hair-pins. Yeah. I was good with that.

CHAPTER
Twenty-Five

THE REST of the weekend blurred into two parallel universes. The official one that everyone involved with the Marcus Foundation saw, and the secret one that Logan and I lived inside our hotel room.

Norman paraded us through small breakout sessions. One with the MacIntyre Foundation, one with a couple of MLAs, another with a gaggle of private-school women who controlled half the city's fundraising committees.

I sat in on discussions about youth pathways in the arts and long-term community engagement, listening to smart things about infrastructure and mentorship. I soaked it all up like a sponge.

Logan sat through media-coaching refreshers and sponsor conversations. He answered questions about the Blizzard mess and why he was interested in the new gallery.

On paper, we were composed and professional. In practice, we could barely keep our hands off each other.

It started small. His knee brushing mine under the dinner table. My hand resting on the back of his chair and lingering longer than necessary. His palm on my back as we squeezed through a crowded foyer, or his thumb tracing a distracting little circle just under my shoulder blade.

I was drunk on all of it. Drunk on him. On the fact that this man who could bulldoze an NHL defenseman with his shoulder would go dead still if I touched the inside of his wrist. That he would excuse himself from a conversation mid-sentence to follow me upstairs if I sent him one well-timed look.

We did our jobs. We showed up. We were brilliant, behaved, and impeccably professional in every meeting scheduled for us. But the second there was a break in the calendar?

Being with Logan was the most fun I'd ever had.

We ordered room service and ate dessert in bed, laughing so hard over some story about training camp that my stomach cramped. We argued over movies and books. We watched half of some terrible late-night sitcom with the volume low, his hand resting over my bare hip like it had always belonged there.

I did my exploring, and he did his. He spent hours that weekend doing exactly what he'd promised and then some.

I never once pretended.

On Sunday, late morning, we packed up the room in a daze.

The drive back down the mountain was quiet. Comfortable. I kept waiting for the regret to hit. The shame. But it didn't.

I was positive it would happen once I got home. Once I saw Maddie and Shar face-to-face. They'd been supportive of this whole thing before, but there was no way in hell I'd be able to explain this.

When we hit the outskirts of Calgary, my stomach started to hollow out. Not because of what had happened, but because of what was about to. Logan would take my exit. He'd drop me at the fourplex, he'd drive home, and we'd both drop back into our regular lives.

The life where we didn't sleep next to each other. Where we couldn't just disappear upstairs for an hour before dinner.

Logan pulled to the right and flicked on his signal. The *click-click-click* echoed in my brain.

"Logan—" I started as he said, "Come to my place?" already pulling out of the turn-only lane.

It was a terrible idea since I had homework to do and didn't have a stitch of clean laundry left in my bag.

Obviously, I said yes.

———

I did eventually go home, and the following week was chaos. School. Work. By day, I had lectures, studio time, and meetings at the gallery. I finalized wall texts and refined the proposed student-programming schedule for submission to Douglas and the provincial grant committee.

By night, more often than not, I was at Logan's. I told Jenna and Lindsey I had a group project. A late shift at the gallery. Over the weekend, I was staying at my parents' to help with holiday baking.

But Jenna and Lindsey weren't idiots. I was happier than I'd ever been, and they knew it wasn't a paycheck or sugar cookie that made the difference.

I should have felt worse about the secret life I was leading, especially when I didn't come clean with Maddie. I did feel guilt in flashes. But then Logan would open his door, hair damp from a shower, wearing sweats and a T-shirt, and everything else would go out the window.

On Sunday night, I lay in his arms, curled against his chest. He'd been quieter than usual, more intense.

"You played so well last night," I murmured, dropping a kiss on his chest.

He blew out a breath. "My positioning was off."

I traced a slow circle around his belly button. I didn't argue. I'd learned not to try and make him feel better about something that frustrated him. Especially when it came to hockey.

Logan threaded his fingers in my hair. "My mom called this morning."

I tilted my head to look at him. "Oh yeah?"

"She asked if we'd stayed in the same room in Banff."

I snorted. "What did you say?"

"I said that was what Norman booked for us. She said . . . she was disappointed in my choices."

I barked a laugh. "She's disappointed? *She's* disappointed?"

Logan wasn't laughing.

I pushed up on one elbow, the sheet slipping down my shoulder. "Logan, you have to call her out on this."

Logan stared at the ceiling. "I grew up thinking they were the ideal. Perfect couple. Dad made the money, Mom stayed home and took me to the zoo, and art museums. She drove me to practices. They both came to all my games."

I didn't interrupt, not wanting to say anything that would spook him from continuing on. For all the vulnerable physical conversations we'd had, there were still a few topics Logan avoided like the plague. This was one of them.

"And now," he said slowly, "I'm looking at them and realizing that for all I know they were faking it the whole time."

I watched him, my heart aching. I didn't have a single thing I could say to make this better. He'd used the word "fake," and that immediately made me think of us. The past few days, I'd tried a couple of times to bring up the gallery opening and what we would look like after. In response, he joked around, teased that at least I wouldn't be so desperate for sex like I thought.

All of it made me feel like my insides had been scooped out. He didn't want to talk about his parents, and he didn't want to talk about us. Which hadn't been a problem until I started being honest with myself. About what I was feeling. What I wanted.

After a few moments, Logan rolled out of bed, grabbing his sweatpants from the floor. "I'm going to the gym."

Now it was my turn to frown. "Is it open this late?"

"Yeah. For another two hours at least."

"You have practice in the morning."

"I know."

"Logan—"

He shoved his legs into the sweats, pulling them up with a rough yank. He'd gone to the gym for an extra workout yesterday, too.

"Don't you think you're pushing yourself a little too hard?"

He shrugged, walking back to the bed to kiss me on the cheek. "I've got to get more explosive on my sprints." He grabbed his keys and was gone a second later, the door clicking shut behind him.

The silence that swooped in was a vacuum. I lay back down on his pillow, breathing in the faint mix of his cologne and detergent.

Logan was nothing if not a hard worker. If something wasn't right, he carved into it with relentless precision until it bent into submission. He fixed everything by doing.

I closed my eyes, forcing my lungs to fill. Less than two weeks, and we'd be walking through the finished gallery together. Less than two weeks, and Logan and I would hit the agreed-upon end point for whatever this was.

Our expiration date was approaching.

My stomach twisted so sharply I had to roll onto my side. Was I really just another drill he was running? Another weak point to strengthen? Another item on a list he could put a checkmark beside once he'd improved enough to move on? That was what we'd agreed upon, wasn't it?

The idea slammed my chest with a two-by-four.

Of course that's what I was—what we were. Logan criticized his parents, but what was the difference between them and us? How could he be angry with his mom and have a real conversation with her when he didn't want anything more than fake?

I swung my legs over the side of the bed and forced my feet

onto the floor. I grabbed my clothes, tugging them on with shaking hands, then shoved my toiletries into my bag, slung my coat over my arm, and ran to the phone.

Tears pricked my eyes as I dialled. There was only one person who knew exactly what I was feeling. Only one person who could snap me out of this, and I couldn't wait another second to talk to her.

Twenty-Six

BY THE TIME I made it to Shar and Rob's front step, my jeans were soaked halfway up my shins, and my eyelashes had tiny ice crystals clinging to them. The snowstorm had rolled in fast. One of those Alberta specials where the sky went from normal to end of days in an hour. The wind clawed at my scarf as I hunched against it, one gloved hand clamped around a Tupperware of cookies I'd brought for them. Jenna made them. She'd picked me up from Logan's, but I insisted on walking to Shar's since Jenna had a paper due in the morning and I wasn't ready to leave right away.

I regretted everything.

I knocked, and Shar opened the door, hair in a messy bun, wearing leggings and one of Rob's oversized hoodies. Warm air spilled out, smelling like fresh bread and oregano.

"What are you doing out in this?" she demanded, grabbing my sleeve and hauling me inside. "You're going to freeze to death."

"To be fair, I didn't know it was going to dump." I held the door open and kicked snow off my shoes. "Also, hi."

I handed her the cookies and got my shoes off, then took off my toque and unwrapped my scarf, avoiding her eyes. When I finally looked up, every emotion inside me rushed forward like the tide.

I clamped my jaw, trying to fight it back, but my eyes still watered, making my nose tingle so bad, I coughed.

Shar dropped the cookies on the side table and pulled me into a hug. "What's wrong?"

"Nothing."

"I call bullshit. What's going on?" She held me while I sobbed into her shoulder, and when I finally pulled back, I didn't have to say anything.

Shar's face fell. "Oh, Crys . . ."

"I didn't mean for it to happen!"

Shar grabbed my hand and pulled me to the couch. We sank onto the cushions, and she handed me a tissue box. Baby toys were scattered on the rug, there was a stack of music scores on the coffee table, and a half-finished mug of tea on the end table, now accompanied by the cookies I brought.

Shar tucked her legs under her. "Okay. Start talking."

So I did. I told her about the late-night phone calls. The reception at the Palliser. Started with the weekend at the Banff Springs hotel and then struggled to explain what had happened that night in our hotel room.

"He said *what?*" Shar's eyes flashed, and I had to talk her down.

Logan hadn't pressured me into anything. He'd never made me feel unsafe or like he wouldn't respect whatever boundaries I set. I wasn't angry with him. I was angry with myself.

"I don't know how I let this happen. I knew from the beginning this was fake. We never pretended it was anything different, but now it's going to end, and I don't think I want it to—" My voice caught, and Shar pulled me into another hug.

She held me for a long moment, until I had to blow my nose so I wouldn't snot all over Rob's sweatshirt.

Shar was quiet. When I finished adding to my pile of tissues on the coffee table, she said, "I'm honestly a little shocked."

"I know. I don't know what I was thinking—"

"No, about Logan."

I wiped my cheeks. "What?"

She looked down at her hands. "Those conversations you're having? He never talked like that with me."

"Shar—"

"No, I'm not upset about it, I'm just surprised. I didn't think he was capable of being that open with someone."

I dropped my head back on the cushions. "It's probably because he knows there's no risk. What am I going to do? Tell everyone? Admit that I forced him into dating me so I could get a job?"

"Okay, that's not fair. You gave him the chance to say no, and I don't think that's what's happening here. The Logan I knew wouldn't have admitted he was bad at sex, ever. I'm not sure it even once crossed his mind." Shar's mouth quirked, and she lowered her voice even though Rob hadn't made an appearance. "You're saying he's good at it now?"

I twisted my head to look at her without lifting it. "Um, yeah. He's good." Good didn't begin to cover it. I dreamed about him. He monopolized my thoughts from the time I woke up until I saw his truck pull up outside my apartment.

Shar's eyes widened. "Well, you must be an excellent teacher."

I half-laughed, half-groaned. "I've created a monster." It was me. The Logan-addicted, Kemp-craving monster was me.

Shar new exactly what I was getting at. "But how do you know he doesn't want the same thing you do?"

I didn't, not specifically. But what was I supposed to do? Tell him I decided I didn't want to honour our end date? We had an agreement, and he'd never said a word to indicate he wasn't planning to abide by it.

"If he did, wouldn't he tell me?" I asked.

Shar considered that. "If you asked me that question a month ago, I would've said absolutely not. But . . . I don't think I know Logan anymore. Not really."

I drew a deep breath and exhaled. "I don't know. He's so open about some things, but then with others, he's completely closed."

"Like what?"

"Like his mom's affair."

Shar's jaw dropped. Oops. Guess I'd left that part out. I filled her in, telling her more details than I'd given Logan since I knew she wouldn't flip her lid.

"Oh, damn."

I nodded. "Yeah. He still hasn't said a word. I see his mom at the gallery, and she just walks around with Norman like everything is completely normal."

Shar sighed. "Okay, see, that Logan I do get."

I waited for Shar to continue.

"I've thought about this a lot, actually," she said, "about what he admitted to me when he came back to the apartment. He said he only knew how to love hockey, and I'm not going to pretend that I know his family well, but from what I've seen, I get it."

I nodded. I thought I knew what she was getting at, but I wanted to hear her explanation. "They seem like they have high expectations."

Shar made a face. "Most parents have high expectations. The problem comes if they don't accept you *unless* you meet them."

"But Logan has met all of their expectations."

"Yeah, I know. And do his parents feel loving to you? Have you met them?"

I let out a breath. "I've only met his dad once. I've seen Alice a few times."

"Well, she's the more warm and fuzzy of the two of them."

Yikes. I thought back to the interactions I'd observed between

Logan and Alice. It wasn't that they were bad, but they felt almost transactional. Like they were work colleagues or associates. When they talked about Logan at the Palliser, it didn't feel loving. Maybe a little like pride, but mostly it felt like they were putting things in order.

"Logan told me they were pretty strict growing up."

"That's one way to put it." Shar scoffed. "Did he tell you what they said to me the first time we met?"

I shook my head.

"His mom said that he had high potential, and if he was going to have God's help getting to the NHL, he needed to keep himself pure."

I nearly choked on my spit.

Shar held up a hand. "And here's the thing, I have no problem with their religious beliefs. What I have a problem with is that she was telling me as if it was my responsibility to make sure he didn't screw up." She reached up and tightened her bun. "It's like they don't see Logan as a real person. He's their action figure. They can pick him up and put him wherever they want, and he'll do what he's told. They don't want anyone else touching him."

I remembered Logan in our hotel room, how he'd responded when I teased him about his parents' approval. "I don't think he wants to play their games anymore."

Shar pursed her lips. "Then why hasn't he called his mom out for cheating?"

I turned to the side, curling into myself on the couch. I'd been asking myself that for the last couple of weeks. "I don't know."

Shar's expression softened. "Crys, Logan's a great guy. He's funny. He's an incredibly hard worker. He's beyond generous. You saw what he did for Rob, letting him live in that apartment rent-free. He's got a good heart. But you know why I think he loves hockey so much?"

I wet my lips. "Because it's in his control."

She nodded. "That's all he's ever been shown. Love doesn't mean letting go or sacrifice. It means something he's good at, something he can predict, something he can check the boxes for and get the exact result he was promised. That's all that's been modelled in the Kemp household."

My throat thickened. "I get that. I do. I've seen it. I know exactly what you're saying. But I think he wants something different. Maybe he just doesn't know how to do it." She studied me. I went on, "Did you know, after you broke up with him, he called his exes?" Her eyes widened. "Yeah. He asked them what he did wrong and how he could fix it."

"But that's exactly it. He's trying to be *good* at a relationship, trying to understand it so he can excel."

My cheeks flamed. That was almost exactly what he'd said to me in the hotel room.

"But when it comes down to it," Sharla continued, "is he going to be willing to take the leap? Put himself on the line? Because you don't want a partner who you can't trust to do the hard things."

She motioned to the hallway. "I thought getting married was scary, but having kids? I'm already messing everything up. Both of us are. Carter's only a month old, and we can't control whether he eats or sleeps. Loving Rob is scary, but loving Carter?" Her voice went soft. "It's like my heart is living outside of my chest. And if Rob wasn't willing to be all in with me? I don't know, Crys."

Tears filled my eyes. Her words wouldn't be making me cry if I didn't know they were true. "So what do I do? Because I think my heart is—" I couldn't finish the sentence.

Shar teared up, reaching for my hand. "I wish I could tell you that it'll all be fine . . . but I walked away because I knew it wouldn't be."

"What would it have taken for you to stay?"

She shook her head. "So many things. But the biggest one? I would've needed to see that he wasn't just worried about making life go smoothly for himself. That when something really mattered, he was willing to take the hit."

"But what would that look like? How would I be able to tell?"

Shar squeezed my hand. "There's a hit he's not willing to take right now, isn't there?"

CHAPTER

Twenty~Seven

ON THE EVENING of December 12th, the gallery walls gleamed in crisp matte white, and the polished floor reflected the warm gold of the overhead fixtures. People were already crowding into the reception area. There were donors in wool coats, Douglas administrators in their formalwear, members of the press, and Blizzard players in outfits that ranged from business casual to custom-tailored suits.

My chest was full to bursting. I'd curled my hair, shaved, and purchased a new dress for this, and it was one-hundred-percent worth it.

I'd helped build this, and it was stunning.

Since it was the press walkthrough and not the official gallery opening, there were still displays in progress. But our featured artist and student artist sections were pristine.

I stopped in front of Bridet's newest piece. A massive canvas in deep reds and icy blues, layered with palette-knife strokes that carved motion into the abstract outline of a player racing down the ice. The flex of the stick, the angle of the blades. It made my heart race.

Alice Kemp's paintings hung in the next section. I'd seen pictures, but standing in front of them was something else. Oil on rough-textured board. Creams, golds, sage green, streaks of dark umber slashed like wounds. My heart twisted because I didn't want to like it, but I did. It was extraordinary.

I forced myself on to inspect the student work I'd helped select. Two pieces stood out under the lights, and there, beside them, was the triptych. Tash's triptych.

I beamed at the three distorted figures mid-stride. Bodies blurring into motion. As compulsive and cutting and brilliant as the first moment I saw them. None of them knew they'd been chosen yet. They'd find out with the rest of Calgary when their names showed up in the paper. Norman would send them an email tomorrow, as well, but he did enjoy a dramatic announcement.

"Proud?" a familiar voice said behind me.

I turned to see Alison Kerr standing at the door. "I'm so happy for them."

Alison stepped into the room. "You had input on these selections."

"I did."

She inspected the pieces, then turned to me and handed me a card. "Call me after graduation. And," she leaned in, "don't tell Norman we had this conversation." She winked and stalked back out of the room.

My head spun, and I almost put out a hand to steady myself, but didn't want to leave any fingerprints. I crouched instead, dropping my head to my knees for a few seconds. Alison Kerr from Glenbow wanted me to call her after graduation.

I stood, hurrying to the main hall. Where was Logan? I needed to—

I pulled to a stop, remembering why I wasn't already at his side. He was with his team, and I was having a hard time pretending.

I took a moment to pull myself together, then walked into the main reception area. The Blizzard players were already gathered around the charcuterie table.

Davis Rourke waved when he saw me. "Hey, Logan was looking for you."

I smiled, flattered that he even remembered who I was. "Hi. So glad you all could come."

He motioned at the spread. "You did this?"

"I helped, but I can't take all the credit."

Another player stepped up. "You're Crystal?" He shook my hand and introduced himself as Jonas, then glanced around the room. "Logan won't shut up about you."

My face heated, and I brushed off the comment. "I doubt that."

He took a bite of salami. "I'm serious. He's a little whipped, if you know what I mean."

A thread of warmth braided through my ribs. Rourke laughed, then pointed out another teammate's plate, and they moved on just as I spotted Logan at the edge of the room.

His suit was black, tailored. His tie was slate grey. His hair was styled, his face clean-shaven. He stood talking to Norman and a few of the people we'd met in Banff. Laughing, his hands gesticulating.

But when he looked up and saw me? His smile softened, his movements slowed. He said something to the others and started toward me.

"Hey," he murmured, leaning close.

"Hey," I said.

"You look incredible." His eyes flicked down my indigo dress, lingering on the deep V cut. Maddie and I found it on clearance at The Bay earlier that week. It was silky and light-weight and combined perfectly with a pair of Jenna's heels. I'd never felt so sexy in my life.

"I still can't get over how good you look in suits."

Logan's smile was wolfish as he brushed a hand down my arm. "I missed you."

He'd been gone on another away tour, and I'd watched every game. I was a glutton for punishment.

He glanced around, then slipped his hand into mine and tugged me toward the back hallway, the one that led to the staff break room and storage.

"Logan," I whispered. "We can't—"

"We won't be long." He pushed open a small utility door and pulled me in with him. The second the door shut, his hands were on my waist, lifting me onto a low storage table. He pushed my already short skirt up and pressed in between my legs. His mouth met mine with a deep, aching hunger that sent shock-waves straight to my middle.

"I missed you," he breathed. "Missed this. Missed—"

I shivered, pulling him closer by the lapels of his suit jacket. "You can't do this to me in public."

"Then stop looking like that in public," he whispered back, kissing down my jaw.

My breath stuttered. Maybe I didn't have to have a conversation with him? Maybe things were fine the way they were. If I left it alone and didn't overthink it, maybe we could—

"Come over tonight." He slid his hand up my thigh.

I sighed against his mouth. "I can't. I have to wake up early for my final."

"But you're going home for Christmas."

I nodded, trying to focus. I was leaving on the sixteenth. "I'll be back on the twenty-sixth." I'd thought about cutting my time short, but everyone was going to be home this year, and my parents had planned a huge staycation. Ten days were barely enough time to pack in all our favourites.

Logan's hands pressed into my back. "Not enough time. We'll only have what, not even two weeks?"

It was as if he'd injected ice water into my veins. "Logan—" He kissed me again, and I pulled back. "Logan, stop. I need to tell you something."

He panted, pressing his forehead to mine. "What is it?"

My heart climbed into my throat. Was I going to do this? Was I going to tell him the truth? If I said these words, there was no way to take them back. But that's what Shar meant, wasn't it? Her heart living outside of her body? If I wasn't willing to take the risk, then how could I expect Logan to?

"This isn't working for me anymore, Logan."

He frowned, pulling back an inch. "Are you . . . did I mix things up? Is this supposed to be our breakup—"

"No, you didn't mix anything up." I put my hand on his cheek. "It's not working for me because . . ." Every cell in my body screamed for me to stop there. To hop off the shelf and make a beeline back to the cheese and sausage. But then I'd be back to sitting at home watching the game and eating a pint of ice cream, drowning in worry and what ifs. I deserved better.

"I care about you," I blurted. "I know this whole thing was supposed to be for show, and all of the physical stuff was purely educational, but it's not fake for me anymore." Once I opened up the dam, I couldn't put the walls back up. "I miss you when I'm not there at your apartment. I think about you all the time. When something happens in the studio, the first person I want to tell is you. You make me laugh, and you make me feel . . . everything." I sucked in a breath, my heart thrumming like a rabbit's. "I don't want to have a breakup date. I want this—you and me—to be real."

Logan's eyes were dark, his breathing slow and controlled. "I'd be good with that. We can keep things exactly as they are."

I shook my head. "No. That's the thing. I don't want them exactly as they are."

"What do you mean?"

My hands went cold. "I mean, I want this to be real, Logan. Not just the fun stuff. We'd need to talk about the things that aren't working."

He frowned. "What's not working? I thought this was good for both of us."

"No, it is, but there are some things we didn't need to deal with when it was temporary."

"Like what?" His voice held an edge, and I knew that look in his eye. It was the same one I'd seen when I pulled him aside near the bathrooms at the Palliser.

"Like the way you shut down and refuse to talk about things when they make you uncomfortable."

He pulled back fully, frustration sparking in his eyes. "So about my mom? You have to let that go."

"It's not only that."

"Pretty sure it is." I pushed off the shelf and grabbed his hand, but he pulled it away. Logan continued, "It has nothing to do with you. Nothing to do with me, either. They're my parents, but they can make their own decisions."

"No, Logan. The decisions they make affect you! When we're in relationships, when we love people, we should expect them to be honest. We have to talk about the hard things and fix our mistakes. Otherwise—" I shook my head. "What's the point? It all might as well be fake."

His mouth flattened. "You don't know my family."

"You're right, but I know what I've seen. What you've told me." I drew a deep breath and pressed my hands to my hips. "What they have . . . it's not what I want. I don't want to avoid the topics that are hard. I don't want to leave things alone because they're going to make someone mad."

"So that's what you think? That because I won't confront my mom, I'd do the same thing to you?"

My mouth went dry. "I don't know, Logan. You tell me. What did your exes have to say?" It was a low blow, but I wasn't getting through to him, and this was the honest truth. Right now, here with me, Logan still didn't want to take the hit.

His jaw worked, and I half-wished he'd lash out. Tell me I had no right to use that against him, and cut me deep like I'd just cut him.

But he didn't.

Logan turned and stalked toward the door, then paused before exiting. "I care about you, too," he murmured. Then slipped into the hall.

It took me a few minutes to follow, my limbs shaky. Grief washed over me in waves. Was that the last time I'd talk to him? Be close to him?

. . . and when that's not good enough, you get over it and move on. End of story.

Tears pricked my eyes as I wove through the patrons, their laughter and clinking wine glasses muted behind the ringing in my ears.

Norman stood at the front near the podium. "Ladies and gentlemen, I just received news."

The crowd hushed.

"I'm pleased to share that as of this afternoon," Norman continued, "the Marcus Arts Foundation has officially secured the full matching grant from the Province of Alberta."

The crowd gasped, then erupted into applause.

The announcement brushed over me, floating behind as I moved faster through the crowd and escaped through the front doors.

CHAPTER
Twenty~Eight

I WOKE up in my own bed, and despite the soft winter light and my warm blankets, I felt anything but comforted. There was no sound of his breathing. No heavy arm slung over my waist. No half-asleep mumble about five more minutes when his alarm went off.

My eyes stung.

I lay there staring at the ceiling, feeling the dull ache under my ribs where last night's conversation had buried itself. I'd done the right thing, but my heart didn't seem to care about long-term ramifications.

I thought about calling him. Apologizing. Taking it all back.

Which is why I nearly had a heart attack when the phone rang to life in the kitchen. I bolted out of bed so fast, I tripped on my sheets and slammed my knees into the floor. Muttering curses, I stumbled out of my room and ran to grab the phone before it went to the answering machine.

"Hello?"

"Hey, hey!" Not Logan. Maddie. I exhaled, half relieved, half disappointed.

"Hey, what's up?" She hesitated, and I filled in the gap. "Shar told you?"

"She only told me that you were having a rough week . . ."

I exhaled, slumping against the counter. "Yeah. Rough night, actually."

"Did you talk with him?"

"I did."

"And?"

I twisted the phone cord around my finger. "Not so great."

Maddie groaned. "I'm sorry."

I fought a second round of tears filling my eyes.

"So . . . trivia tonight at The Den?"

I blinked, sniffing as I spun to look at the calendar. "It's Friday."

"It's Friday," Maddie said. "Pick you up at seven?"

"Yes, please."

———

The Den at the U of C was hopping. It was already decorated for Christmas with holiday lights strung over and around the bar and tinsel tacked on the trivia host's mic stand. Maddie snagged us a high-top near the right edge of the trivia section, close enough to the speakers to hear questions, far enough that we'd still be able to hear each other talk.

She brandished one of the pencils sitting next to our answer sheet. "Team name?"

"The Comeback Queens," I said. The last time we'd been here, we annihilated the competition. It was high time we defended our title.

She cackled. "I love it. Perfect."

We ordered nachos and ginger ales, because I didn't trust my emotional state with anything stronger, and settled in as the trivia host explained the rules. We spotted some of the regulars around the room and waved, but there were plenty of new faces, too.

"Okay, tonight's theme for Round One is . . ." The host paused for dramatic effect, flipping his cue card like he was revealing a game-show prize. "Holiday Movies!"

Maddie perked up like someone had plugged her into a generator. "Oh, we're about to destroy."

"Agreed." This was one category I had plenty of experience with.

The host continued, "Question number one: In what 1990 Christmas classic does an eight-year-old boy defend his home from burglars after his family accidentally leaves him behind for the holidays?"

Maddie and I exchanged a look. "Oh, c'mon," she said, scribbling in Home Alone.

As the round went on, the questions ramped up from nostalgic comfort shows to only-people-who-lived-in-the-video-rental-section-know-this. The host dove into supporting characters, production trivia, original release posters. Maddie hit her first wall when he asked, "In the 1988 film *Scrooged*, what's the name of the network's live Christmas special that Frank Cross forces everyone to produce?"

She blinked at me, but I was grinning from ear to ear. I grabbed the sheet and wrote: *A Christmas Carol: Scrooge LIVE!*

Maddie stared. "How—why—how do you have that stored in your head?"

I shrugged. "You know math. My family knows Bill Murray."

We won round one, though our score was barely higher than the table across from us. A victory, nonetheless.

Between rounds, we talked Christmas.

"What's your plan?" I asked, popping a jalapeño popper into my mouth.

"Going home for actual Christmas Day," she said.

"Both of you?"

Maddie nodded. "It'll be interesting."

I grinned. "Will your mom let you share a room?"

She snorted. "She's still so paranoid that something happened between the two of us in high school. I don't know what I'd need to do to convince her."

I laughed. "Probably just start making up stories. Specifically about times when she wasn't home."

Maddie clutched her stomach. "She'd kill me!"

We ate and started round two on American Presidents, and Maddie told me about Chase's plans for New Year's. The Hitmen were doing some charity skate on New Year's day, but they didn't have specific plans for New Year's Eve.

It was exactly what I'd hoped to hear. "My parents are throwing a party. Neighbours, friends. We'll have appetizers, drinks, and games. You and Chase should come."

She blinked. "They'd be okay with that?"

"Of course. It'll be fun. Rob and Shar are invited, too. My parents are dying to see Carter."

Maddie considered. "That actually sounds amazing."

I was beyond grateful. Having something to look forward to now that any plans outside of my family seemed to be obsolete meant more to me than Maddie or Shar could've possibly known.

I took a sip of my ginger ale. "Thank you. For setting this up."

Maddie winked. "Family, babe. Don't ever forget it."

The last week of the semester went by in a blur.

Final papers. Studio clean-up. Last critiques. Shar's holiday concert.

At the gallery, things ramped up instead of down. We had a

small media event with the selected Douglas students. We did photos and a short Q&A about the emerging artist component of the Marcus Foundation program.

"You did this," Tash whispered, squeezing my hand. "You got me up on that wall."

"You did this," I corrected. "I didn't know it was you when I voted."

Norman hovered in the background, smiling his benevolent-founder smile, talking to reporters about investment in the next generation. More than once I looked for Logan on the off-chance he'd show up, but I didn't even see Alice there.

And, strangely enough, her featured artist wall was empty. Had they decided to switch out the art? Showcase another piece for the official gallery opening?

I wanted to ask him about it. I wanted to know how he was doing after the Blizzard lost to the Avalanche. Whether Rourke was okay since he left after a bad hit and didn't return to the bench.

I had so many questions. But Logan hadn't called.

That night, I packed. My suitcase lay open on my bed, my clothes in a pile that looked like a thrift store explosion. I folded sweaters, stuffed socks into boots, and put all my dirty laundry in a trash bag to wash at home so I didn't have to use our communal machines.

My dad showed up the next morning, and we drove away from campus. We passed the gallery on the way out of town. The parking lot was empty.

Somewhere, Logan was on a bus or a plane or a hotel bed, stretching tired muscles, taping his stick.

"If you're cold, you can hit the button right there." My dad pointed to the dash. "This model has heated seats."

I blinked, turning away from the window and flicked my seat warmer to high.

CHAPTER
Twenty~Nine

THE MACMILLAN HOUSE at Christmas was a full-sensory experience, and despite everything I'd been feeling, the second I stepped inside and smelled the cinnamon and pine, my whole body exhaled.

My mother, as predicted, had already gone into her annual holiday overachiever mode. Garland snaked around every banister, candles illuminated every window, and a wreath adorned every surface that could hold a nail. The living room showcased our tree with mismatched ornaments from our childhood and my grandmother's hand-knitted stockings.

My parents greeted me with hugs first, and I clung to them a little longer than normal. Connor, my brother, came skidding down the hallway in socks, nearly wiping out, and the rest of my siblings followed.

Within two hours, I'd eaten two bowls of stew, half a loaf of homemade bread, three cookies, and a small bowl of chocolate pudding Dad had insisted I "just try." I slept almost twelve hours that night. When I woke up, I still missed Logan.

———

. . .

Over the following days, we whirled through our holiday plans, visiting the zoo, the science museum, ice skating at the rink in TD Square near the Devonian Gardens, and hitting up Roller-land. Then Christmas Eve arrived fast and furious.

Mom made tourtière because she insisted our family had French-Canadian roots despite no one being able to confirm the genealogy. We ate roast beef and mashed potatoes, and had our traditional Christmas Eve movie marathon, which started with *It's a Wonderful Life* (Dad cried, again), moved to *White Christmas* (Lisa mocked the costumes, again), and ended with *How the Grinch Stole Christmas*. I voted for Rudolph, but Connor still thought the claymation was creepy.

Exchanging presents on Christmas Day was lovely, and eating our breakfast buffet for lunch provided enough calories for the entire week. My mom sent me home with way too many leftovers, and Jenna and Lindsey were more than happy to help me use them up.

While I was beyond grateful for the time with my family, it only made my own apartment feel emptier. In an attempt not to be lonely and pathetic, one night I bundled up and headed to Tash's place, where she and our art-school friends were hosting a White Elephant party with mulled wine and mandatory thrift store Christmas sweaters.

On December twenty-ninth, I gave in and called Logan. When I got his answering machine, I didn't leave a message.

The Outlaws hosted a kegger at Rory and Axel's, but I couldn't bring myself to go. Instead, I passed the next two days braless, enjoying the last of my mom's sausage rolls along with my peanut butter and crackers.

On the afternoon of New Year's Eve, I drove over to the house early with Maddie and Chase to prep appetizers. The house smelled like garlic and puff pastry and the sugar cookies Connor was decorating with far too many sprinkles.

Maddie and Chase jumped fully into the chaos. Chase was gamely letting Connor quiz him on random facts about the NHL while Maddie arranged crackers on a platter. I was chopping cilantro when Mom sidled up beside me.

"How's Logan?" she asked.

My knife slipped and nearly took off a fingertip. "Fine, I think."

Maddie looked up from the crackers.

"Hm." Mom dipped her finger in the sweet chilli mayo she was mixing and tasted. "Ooh, that's good."

She put the lid on the jar and slid it into the fridge. "Did you invite him?"

I frowned. "Who?"

"Logan." Connor answered. He had a knack for eaves-dropping.

The cilantro leaves were becoming less diced and more shredded. "He's pretty busy this time of year with the team." Complete lie. Logan had complained about how I would be gone for so much of the break.

I hadn't formally announced anything, and with the press walk-through over and done with, I didn't feel the need to. There were enough stories popping up over the holidays that nobody cared about Logan Kemp's art student girlfriend.

But I would still have to tell my family and friends. "Actually, that's not completely true. I haven't talked with Logan—"

"Because he's been in Toronto," Maddie cut in. I blinked, my mouth hanging open.

"Oh yeah!" Connor set the sprinkles on the counter with a rattle. "Did he get to do Christmas with his family?"

"Probably." Maddie grinned.

"But if he didn't, they're paying him a shit-ton of money," Chase murmured, and Maddie shot him a look.

Connor was oblivious. He started going off on the game, how it had gone into overtime and then a shoot out.

What was happening right now? I stared at Maddie, willing her to give me some kind of explanation, but we were interrupted by the doorbell.

Shar and Rob arrived along with baby Carter, who looked like a completely different baby.

"He grew," I said, stunned as Rob lifted him from his carseat.

Shar laughed. "Insane, right?"

The guests kept coming, and I jumped into hostess mode, taking drink orders and transporting trays to the table. The house filled with laughter and chatter layered over the Christmas music my parents played on my old boombox.

Midnight grew closer, and my dad started handing out hats and noisemakers. It was my perfect chance to escape. I drifted to the kitchen under the pretense of checking on the cheese platter, then hurried down the hall and slipped into the den, closing the door behind me.

I sank to the floor, dropping my head between my knees. Tomorrow was January 1st. A new year. On paper, every wild dream I'd hoped for had come true for me this holiday season. I had a connection with my art idol, a padded resume, and a veritable job offer come spring. I was no longer staring potential grad school in the face, and I felt more confident than ever before in my ability to transition from campus life to the real world.

But none of it touched the hollow ache sheltered beneath my ribs. Over Christmas, I'd convinced myself that he wasn't calling because he knew I wasn't home. Because he needed time to think through everything.

Now, there was no excuse, and the realization that Logan might not be calling because for him it was only ever fake felt like stepping backward into ice water. My body went numb in sections, one part at a time.

When he said yes to our scheme? It was only for his PR clause. When he got all hot and bothered with Jake? He was only trying to be the alpha. When he told the guys to get me food to earn their Blizzard tickets, it was for fun, not because he cared.

When he suggested we add benefits to our arrangement? It was only for education, like he said in the first place.

Logan had been perfectly clear from the get-go, and Shar had warned me from the start. I was the stupid one. So desperate that I fell into a trap that wasn't even set for me.

I swiped at my cheeks, ignoring the sound of my name coming from the other room. Headlights swept across the snow through the window, and I reached up to flick off the lights. I didn't need some neighbour peering in and seeing me huddled up on the floor.

A car door slammed.

"Crystal?" It was my dad's voice. I prayed that he wouldn't come looking.

Heavy steps sounded on the porch, and I frowned. It was too dark to see the clock, but it had to be eleven-thirty.

The doorbell rang. Who was showing up to the party this late?

Stomps down the hall.

Jingle bells ringing as the door swung open.

Then a low voice. A laugh.

And Connor's excited whoop from the living room. "Logan freaking Kemp!"

CHAPTER
Thirty

I SCRAMBLED TO MY FEET, heart pounding so hard it rattled my teeth. *Logan was here?* I spun in a circle, not sure how I could escape without being noticed.

The den door creaked, and I yelped.

Maddie and Sharla barreled in, closing the door behind them.

"What are you doing sitting here in the dark?" Sharla hissed.

"What do you think I'm doing? I was crying in peace!"

Maddie scoffed. "We've been looking for you, trying to tell you Logan was coming!"

"You knew?!" My voice was louder than I intended, and Sharla hushed me.

Excited chatter sounded from the hall. Connor was saying something about Logan signing his goalie stick. My dad said no since it was only twenty minutes until the countdown.

"How did you know Logan was coming?" I was not letting them off the hook with this one.

"We didn't know for sure," Sharla insisted. "He was travelling back with the Blizzard, and we weren't sure if he'd make it in time."

"But you talked to him?"

Maddie nodded. "I was over at Shar's on Boxing Day. Logan stopped by."

My eyes had to be bugging out of my head.

"Uh, I think they'll be back in just a second." Rob's voice. It sounded as if he was walking closer to us.

"You need to get out there!" I pushed them both toward the door.

"But—"

Maddie didn't get the chance to finish her argument because the door to the den swung open, light from the hall pouring in on all three of us huddled together.

Rob, Chase and Logan mirrored us over the threshold. "Never mind. Found them."

"WHY ARE you three lurking in there like raccoons?" Rob asked, Carter wrapped in his arms.

Maddie and Shar exited as Shar said, "We're not lurking, we were checking on something."

"It's pitch black in there," Rob started, but I was no longer paying attention to their conversation.

Logan stood in front of me, blocking most of the light from the living room. He wore jeans and a light hoodie.

For a heartbeat, we stared at each other, neither moving. Then Logan asked, "Can I come in?"

I nodded, stepping back so he could enter. He closed the door behind him. The den fell back into darkness, lit only by the glow from the streetlights. The room felt too small. Like my bedroom that first night he'd shown up.

I almost asked how he'd gotten my address, but if Shar and Maddie had talked with him, I'd put all my marbles on them. Logan stepped further into the room and sat down on the edge of the futon.

I couldn't sit. My body was all restless energy and jangling nerves. I needed to move, or I was going to explode. So I paced toward the window, then to the desk where I parked, leaning against the scroll-top.

"How have you been?" he asked quietly.

The question was so ordinary it almost made me laugh. Like we were classmates bumping into each other in the hallway after midterms, not two people who'd seen every part of each other and then spent two weeks pretending the other didn't exist.

I thought about continuing the ruse. *Fine. Busy.* Instead, I gave in to the pressure pounding in my head and said, "Not great."

He looked up. "Crystal—"

"You never called," I cut in, heat rushing up my throat. "After the gallery. After I told you I cared about you. Nothing. No call. No email." He flinched, barely, but I was on a roll. "I stepped off a cliff in front of you, and your response was nothing. Silence. Do you have any idea how that felt? To be here, with my family, pretending everything's fine while you're out there—" I gestured vaguely. "I don't know, doing whatever the hell you were doing? I—"

"Crys, you were right." His jaw flexed, his fingers curling together.

The words landed like a brick in a still pond, ripples racing from the impact. My mouth snapped shut.

He let out a long breath, shoulders sagging. "You were right about me. And about my family. I think I've been faking relationships my whole life."

Logan waited for that to sink in before continuing. "I know it probably seemed like that's what it was with you. But it wasn't." He scrubbed a hand over his face. "I was lonely—"

"Well, I was too."

He nodded. "But even when I started making friends with guys on the team, I still wanted to call you. To be with you. It wasn't about what I could get away with or what image I could maintain. I didn't—" He leaned back, dropping his hands on his knees. "I lied to you, Crys."

My breathing slowed. "About what?" I braced myself for impact.

"That whole thing about my mom telling Norman about us. I made it up."

I frowned. "Why?"

His fingers twitched on his jeans. "Because I asked her if we could get a meeting set up, and she said no. She didn't want to use that connection for something that wasn't important, but she'd already volunteered me for his outreach, so . . . I told her I wouldn't do it. Unless my girlfriend could get an intro. I tried saying you were just a friend, and then she couldn't understand why that would be so important to me, so I made it up."

I took that in, thinking back to that night at the gallery. How his mom had taken him outside the tent. "So Norman offering me the job—"

"Had nothing to do with me. But I thought I was just getting you the intro—"

"And you didn't know that lie would last."

He nodded, and the pieces clicked into place. Why he'd been so eager to come over to my place. Why he hadn't even blinked when I told him that I'd signed the contract.

I pushed off the desk, pacing in front of him. "But you didn't have to stick with it. As soon as I told you I signed the contract, you could've told me. We both would've still gone to the events and . . ." I stopped and looked at him. "Why didn't you call it off?"

His Adam's Apple bobbed. "Because I didn't want to stop talking with you."

"We still could've talked."

He scoffed. "You weren't my biggest fan, if you remember."

That was true. Would I have spent time with him had I not believed I'd gotten him into that mess? "So you coming to the gallery—"

"I wanted to be there."

"And picking me up when Jenna's car died."

"Wanted to."

"And the hotel room?" My mouth went dry.

Logan cleared his throat. "Definitely wanted to."

I turned toward the desk, dragging my fingers through my hair. "Then why did you keep talking about January? Why did you say—?"

I gasped as Logan's hands circled my waist. He turned me to face him. "Because you were right." He lifted a hand and smoothed the hair from my cheek.

"I like that you keep saying that."

He chuckled, his hand resting between my neck and my shoulder. "I didn't want to be the one to take the risk."

My breath came in short gasps. I recounted our conversation in the supply closet at the gallery. Everything Logan was saying, it was exactly what I'd hoped for. But Shar's words came crashing into my head. *There's a hit he's not willing to take right now, isn't there?*

"Logan—"

"I talked to my mom. About her and Norman. About the affair. About how long it had been going on. I told her she could tell my dad, or I could, but it wasn't staying a secret."

The room seemed to tilt under my feet. "When?"

"The night of the press walk through."

My eyes widened. *That night?* "What happened?"

"She left," he said simply. "Not permanently, I don't think. But she left the house. Said she needed space. He—" Logan's jaw tightened. "My dad didn't take it well."

"What about Norman?"

Logan pursed his lips. "He might've been fine if my dad hadn't shown up at the gallery and slashed my mom's paintings."

I gasped. "He didn't."

"He sure did."

I laughed out of shock. "I'm sorry, that's not funny."

"It's kind of funny."

"A little sad though. Those paintings were amazing."

Logan nodded. "My mom showed up. Cleaned the mess. I've never seen her so calm."

"Is your dad still—?" I wanted to say having a mental break, but didn't think that was helpful.

Logan's mouth twisted. "He's a mess. Angry. Hurt. He keeps trying to pretend nothing's wrong as long as he can until he explodes. We still haven't had a real conversation about it."

"I'm sorry," I whispered, wondering if all this was my fault. Until I remembered I wasn't the one kissing Norman Marcus in his office.

"But I talked to my mom," Logan went on. "Really talked. For the first time in . . . probably ever. About how their marriage has been hard for years. She felt like she had to be the spiritual glue for all of us, and somewhere along the line, she forgot she was allowed to want anything."

"One minute!" My dad's voice filtered through the closed door.

Logan's throat worked. "I'm sorry I didn't call. It was a lot—"

"No, I totally understand."

"I still should've called. I just wasn't—" He drew in a shaky breath. "I've never missed anyone like this. Not a teammate. Not an ex. Not anyone. I don't want to go on road trips without you, and I know that's ridiculous, but every away game, every hotel room, every bus seat—I just sit there thinking about how I wish you were there next to me."

His hand tensed against my neck. "This scares the shit out of me."

I nodded, sliding my hands around his waist. "Yeah. I know the feeling."

Logan made a noise in his throat, his fingers trembling. "Crys. I—" He took another second, composing himself. "I don't think I've ever said this and meant it, but—"

"TWENTY! NINETEEN!" The countdown started in the other room.

"I love you." Logan's voice splintered. "You said you cared about me at the gallery, and I don't know if that's the same, but I needed you to know that's how I feel. And I get that I still have a lot of work to do. I'm probably still going to be an ass sometimes, and I wish that wasn't true, but I'm going to keep asking questions, and—"

I pressed my fingers to his lips.

"ELEVEN! TEN!"

Logan's eyes lifted, landing on mine. He looked terrified. Desperate. Because he'd just stepped off the edge of the cliff with me.

"I love you, Logan."

He kissed my fingers.

"SEVEN! SIX!"

"I want to be at every game, every tournament, every bus ride."

"FOUR! THREE!"

"I don't expect you to be perfect because I sure as hell won't be. I just want you and—"

Logan was kissing me as my family screamed, "ONE!" and the noisemakers and poppers exploded along with the shouts of "HAPPY NEW YEAR!"

I grabbed the front of his hoodie and pulled him closer. He made a startled sound against my mouth—a half-laugh, half-groan—and then his hands were everywhere. Dragging me back. Pulling me onto his lap as he fell back on the futon.

I nipped his lower lip, running my hands through his hair, wishing I could magically transport us back to his condo because whatever we could do on the other side of this door, it was not going to be enough.

Logan's hands slipped up the back of my shirt, and he smiled. "Three clasps?"

"Comfort bra. I didn't know you were coming."

He laughed, toying with it until I slapped his hands away. "My parents are out there."

"Does this door have a lock?" He picked me up and set me on the cushion, ignoring my protests, and just as he reached for the handle, the door to the den flew open.

Logan jumped back as the overhead light flashed on.

My dad stood in the doorway. "Huh. Why'd you have the lights off?"

I blinked, waiting for it to click in.

My dad, completely oblivious, grinned at Logan. "How about this weekend. Quite the comeback, eh?"

He was talking about the game against Toronto. Connor had filled us all in on Logan's shootout goal in overtime.

Logan glanced at me before turning back to my dad. He coughed a laugh. "You have no idea."

———

NEXT IN SERIES: CANADIAN PLAYED

For an eight book epilogue to Campus Confessions, read Canadian Played, the story of the Snowballs. An Elite League team in Calgary captained by Sharla and Rob's son, Sean. In Book 8, The Dying Seconds, the whole gang is back together to celebrate Rob and Shar's anniversary. You can't miss it!

Start with Against the Boards

Tropes:
- Fake Dating
- Brother's Teammate
- Forced Proximity
- Workplace Romance

Start reading now!

***

Want to connect with me and read books as I write them? Join my Reader's Club!

Cindy Gunderson is a voice actress and award-winning author. Since she has commitment issues, she writes both sci-fi and fantasy, as well as contemporary romance and women's fiction under the pen name, Cynthia Gunderson.

When she is not typing away in a quiet corner of her local library, you can find her traveling with her family, narrating audiobooks, or happily digging in her garden. She loves acting and performing, beating her kids in card games, and playing ultimate frisbee with her handsome husband, Scott.

Cindy grew up in Alberta, Canada, but has lived most of her adult life between California and Colorado. She currently resides in the Denver metro area. Cindy holds a B.S. in Psychology from Brigham Young University.

Cindy's first novel Tier 1 was awarded First Place in Science Fiction at the 2021 CIPPA EVVY Awards and her women's fiction novel Yes, And was honored with the Indie Author Award's first place prize for the state of Colorado, 2023.

Also by Cynthia Gunderson

Standalone Novels

Yes, And, I Can't Remember, Let's Try This Again, Holly Bough Cottage,
The New Year's Party

Sugar Creek Series

One Last Christmas, Love in Audio

Canadian Played Series

Against the Boards, Called for Icing, Stickhandle with Care, On the
Power Play, Guarding Home Ice, Offside Attraction, Drop the Mitts, The
Dying Seconds

Campus Confessions Series

The Breakaway, The Save, The Comeback

Smash Point Social

The Big Dink, The Setup

Find signed books and discounted bundles at

www.CindyGunderson.com

Instagram: @CindyGWrites

Facebook: @CindyGWrites

TikTok: @CynthiaGWrites